LA BOUTIQUE

Francis Durbridge

WILLIAMS & WHITING

Cover design by Timo Schroeder

9781912582426

Williams & Whiting (Publishers)
15 Chestnut Grove, Hurstpierpoint,
West Sussex, BN6 9SS

Titles by Francis Durbridge to be published by Williams & Whiting

A Case For Paul Temple
A Game of Murder
A Man Called Harry Brent
A Time of Day
Bat Out of Hell
Breakaway – The Family Affair
Breakaway – The Local Affair
Death Comes to the Hibiscus (stage play – writing as Nicholas Vane)
La Boutique
Melissa
My Friend Charles
Paul Temple and the Alex Affair
Paul Temple and the Canterbury Case (film script)
Paul Temple and the Conrad Case
Paul Temple and the Curzon Case
Paul Temple and the Geneva Mystery
Paul Temple and the Gilbert Case
Paul Temple and the Gregory Affair
Paul Temple and the Jonathan Mystery
Paul Temple and the Lawrence Affair
Paul Temple and the Madison Mystery
Paul Temple and the Margo Mystery
Paul Temple and the Spencer Affair
Paul Temple and the Sullivan Mystery
Paul Temple and the Vandyke Affair
Paul Temple and Steve
Paul Temple Intervenes
Portrait of Alison
Send for Paul Temple (radio serial)

Send for Paul Temple (stage play)
Step In The Dark
The Broken Horseshoe
The Desperate People
The Doll
The Other Man
The Scarf
The Teckman Biography
The World of Tim Frazer
Three Plays for Radio Volume 1
Three Plays for Radio Volume 2
Tim Frazer and the Salinger Affair
Tim Frazer and the Mellin Forrest Mystery
Twenty Minutes From Rome
Two Paul Temple Plays for Radio
Two Paul Temple Plays for Television

Also by Francis Durbridge and published by Williams & Whiting:

Murder At The Weekend
Murder In The Media

Also published by Williams & Whiting:

Francis Durbridge : The Complete Guide
By Melvyn Barnes

INTRODUCTION

As an enthusiast and researcher of Francis Durbridge (1912-98), the first question I must address is - why publish now the script of his 1967 radio serial *La Boutique*?

The answer is simply that the BBC has never produced CDs of the original production, although this was done for many of Durbridge's other radio serials. The consequence is that many of today's Durbridge fans, depending upon their age, have lacked the opportunity to hear it in English, whereas various European radio translations of *La Boutique* were marketed as CDs – thus cementing the impression that Durbridge might have been more highly appreciated outside his own land.

So at long last this book uniquely reproduces the original UK version of a radio serial that enthralled listeners throughout the world. *La Boutique*, written by Francis Durbridge and produced by Martyn C. Webster (Durbridge's regular radio producer since the 1930s), was first broadcast on BBC Radio 2 from 2 October to 16 October 1967 (two episodes per week) in five thirty-minute episodes. And although it was repeated on BBC Radio 4 from 16 May to 13 June 1968 in weekly episodes, the recording has not since then been made available in any medium in English.

But it might be unwise to assume that everyone reading this is already familiar with Francis Durbridge's career, in which case some background information might be helpful. He bestrode the media as the most popular writer of mystery thrillers for BBC radio and television from the 1930s to the 1970s, after which he enjoyed a successful career as a stage dramatist. His popularity has endured, with his radio serials being regularly repeated in recent years and appearing as CDs, many of his television serials being marketed as DVDs, his novels being frequently reprinted, and his stage plays remaining among the staple fare of amateur and professional companies.

Although he had been writing sketches, stories and plays for the BBC since 1933, it was in 1938 that Francis Durbridge found the niche in which he was to carve his name, when his radio serial *Send for Paul Temple* was a great success and his sequels over several decades built an enormous UK and European fanbase. But by the 1950s it was not only his radio serials that had earned him an enviable reputation, because from 1952 he became the master of thriller serials on BBC television with complex plots and cliff-hanger endings that attracted record viewing figures. Placing him in context, on BBC radio Durbridge vied for many years with fellow thriller writers Edward J. Mason, Lester Powell, Ernest Dudley, Alan Stranks and Philip Levene; while on BBC television it was acknowledged that his serials attracted viewers in numbers that could only compare with those following the *Quatermass* science fiction serials of Nigel Kneale.

By the mid-1960s many European countries had long been broadcasting Durbridge serials in their own languages with their own actors, both for radio and television, and he had become something of a phenomenon. German commentators famously labelled his serials *straßenfeger* (street sweepers), because so many people stayed at home to listen to them on the radio or watch them on television. So undoubtedly he reached the pinnacle of appeal as a radio and television writer throughout Europe – and there is evidence that substantial enthusiasm for Durbridge on the Continent endures today, which makes *La Boutique* rather significant.

This international commission for Durbridge in 1967 earned him the distinction of being the first author invited by the European Broadcasting Union to write a radio serial for multi-lingual broadcasting. The rest is history, with *La Boutique* broadcast throughout Europe – examples being

Austria, Italy, Germany, Belgium, Norway, Sweden, Switzerland, Turkey, Greece and Finland – and even gripping radio audiences in Australia, New Zealand, Canada, South Africa and Japan.

Many of the original UK cast members of *La Boutique* had for some years been associated with Durbridge/Webster radio productions – and in particular Simon Lack (1915-80), who played Superintendent Robert Bristol, appeared in nine of the ten Paul Temple radio serials broadcast from 1955 to 1968, the only exception being *Paul Temple and the Conrad Case* (1959). But there was also the familiar brogue of Duncan McIntyre (1907-73), playing Sergeant Edwards, who acted in nine Temple cases between 1944 and 1968; while Tommy Duggan (1909-98), playing Rolf Winter, had been in eight of them between 1946 and 1961. In addition both McIntyre and Duggan had appeared frequently over several decades in non-Temple radio plays and serials written by Durbridge and produced by Webster.

Among the many European productions of *La Boutique* were the 1967 German translation by Marianne de Barde, produced by Dieter Munck, with Karl Michael Vogler as Robert, Ursula Dirichs as Eve and Wolfgang Weiser as Lewis; the 1968 Swiss production, translated and produced by Hans Hausmann, with René Deltgen as Robert, Maria Magdalena Thiesing as Eve and Maximilian Wolters as Lewis; and the 1968 Italian production, translated by Amleto Micozzi and produced by Umberto Benedetto, with the character names changed.

But to conclude, it is interesting to see how *La Boutique* slotted into the Durbridge oeuvre, for he was a truly multi-media writer. On BBC radio, *La Boutique* (2 October to 16 October 1967) was preceded by the serial *Paul Temple and the Geneva Mystery* (11 April – 16 May 1965) and succeeded by the serial *Paul Temple and the Alex Affair* (26 February –

21 March 1968). On BBC television, the mid-1960s saw his serials *A Game of Murder* (26 February – 2 April 1966) and *Bat Out of Hell* (26 November – 24 December 1966). October 1967 saw the publication of his novel *My Wife Melissa*, on the theatrical stage he had been active since 1964 in Germany, while in the UK his daily newspaper strip *Paul Temple* had been running since 1950 and would continue until 1971.

So *La Boutique* is vintage Durbridge – enjoy!

Melvyn Barnes
Author of Francis Durbridge: The Complete Guide (Williams & Whiting, 2018)

LA BOUTIQUE

A New Play, in five parts,
Specially written for the European Broadcasting Union

By FRANCIS DURBRIDGE

Broadcast on BBC Radio 2
2 October – 16 October 1967
Produced by MARTYN C. WEBSTER

CAST:

Robert Bristol . . . . Simon Lack

Det -Sgt Cooper . . . . Antony Viccars

Hilda . . . . Carol Marsh

Chief Insp Daly . . . . Haydn Jones

Vanessa Allen . . . . Barbara Mitchell

Lewis Bristol . . . . William Fox

Eve Bristol . . . . .Isabel Dean

Katherine Hauptman . . . . .Noel Hood

Freddie Hauptman . . . . Frank Henderson

Mrs Webb . . . . .Beatrice Kane

Det -Sgt Edwards . . . . Duncan McIntyre

Pearl Mortimer . . . . Margaret Robertson

Carl May . . . . Ronald Herdman

Morgan . . . . .Alan Dudley

Dr Underdown . . . . Humphrey Morton

Rolf Winter . . . . .Tommy Duggan

Elka Nelson . . . . Dorit Welles

Hardy (Berry) Nelson . . . . .Jon Rollason

Simone Duprez . . . . Yvonne Andre

Other parts played by Madi Hedd, Beth Boyd and
members of the BBC Drama Repertory Company

This book reproduces Francis Durbridge's original script together with the list of characters and actors of the BBC programme on the dates mentioned, but the eventual broadcast might have edited Durbridge's script in respect of scenes, dialogue and character names.

Part One

Announcements. Music.

Fade Music.

Fade in: typewriter. It stops as the office door opens.

COOPER: Excuse me! Is Superintendent Bristol about?

HILDA: No, I'm afraid he isn't. He's on leave. He won't be back at Scotland Yard for three weeks.

COOPER: Oh, lord …

Door opens.

DALY: Hilda, when you've finished typing that report I want you to … Yes, what is it, Sergeant?

COOPER: There's a cable for Superintendent Bristol, sir. It's from Los Angeles, from someone called Lewis. It came through to the general office.

DALY: (*Impatiently*) Well – what is it? What's it say?

COOPER: (*Reading cable*) "Arrive Savoy tomorrow night. Must see you. Lewis."

DALY: (*After a momentary hesitation*) Er – yes, all right, Cooper. Leave it with me. I'm seeing the Superintendent at lunch-time.

COOPER: (*Relieved*) Thank you, Inspector.

Door closes.

HILDA: (*Surprised*) I thought Superintendent Bristol was in Venice?

DALY: No; he's flying out on Wednesday. Have you finished that report, Hilda?

HILDA: Nearly. I've only two more pages to do.

DALY: Good. (*Thoughtfully; looking at the cable*) "Arrive Savoy tomorrow night." That brother of his must be loaded.

HILDA: Brother?

DALY: Yes – you've heard of Lewis Bristol? The composer.

3

HILDA: (*Surprised*) Lewis Bristol! Is he the Superintendent's brother?

DALY: Yes.

HILDA: Good Lord, I never knew that! The man who wrote "Golden Girl"?

DALY: That's right. He wrote two or three musicals and then went to America. He's been living in Hollywood for the past five years.

HILDA: Have you met him?

DALY: I've shaken hands with him. He was over here about three years ago when he wife divorced him.

HILDA: Well, I'm crazy about his music, I must say. What's he like?

DALY: Oh – stacks of charm. Good looking. Expensive after-shave lotion. You know the type.

HILDA: I don't. I wish I did.

Daly laughs.

HILDA: I suppose he's older than the Superintendent?

DALY: Yes; must be ten years older. He's forty-six at least.

HILDA: Well, he doesn't sound very much like "our Robert".

DALY: They're as different as chalk and cheese. You'd never believe they were brothers. I've met the sister too. Katherine. She's another charmer; but I liked her better than Lewis, I must say.

HILDA: She's the one that married a Swiss – the hotel keeper.

DALY: That's right. They have a hotel in Venice; on the Grand Canal. I've seen pictures of it. Fabulous looking place.

HILDA: Is that where the Super's staying?

DALY: I imagine so.

4

HILDA: Some people have all the luck. <u>My</u> sister married a bus driver.

DALY: I know – and Auntie Hilda's the baby-sitter.

HILDA: You can say that again! Three nights a week … (*Starts typing again*) Baby sucker, if you ask me …

Typing continues.
Fade.

ROBERT: (<u>*Fade in*</u>) … Lewis, I've been here precisely an hour! We've discussed your last show, your next show, your tax problems, what you said to the President of Metro Goldwyn …

LEWIS: (*Laughing*) Good heavens, have I been talking about myself all the time! My dear Robert, I do apologise.

ROBERT: Lewis, you always talk about yourself! I'm not complaining. But I do wish you'd get to the point. Why did you send me that cable? What is it you want me to do?

LEWIS: I want you to help me, Robert.

ROBERT: Well, I will if I can. You know that. But I'd better warn you, if it's anything to do with Eve …

LEWIS: It's nothing to do with Eve! Nothing whatsoever. Good God, are you still carrying a torch for that ex-wife of mine?

ROBERT: (*Annoyed*) Look, Lewis, just because I thought Eve had a raw deal it doesn't mean to say that I …

LEWIS: (*Interrupting*) This isn't anything to do with Eve! Now don't let's get our wires crossed. Don't let's dig up the past, please!

ROBERT: What is it you want me to do?

5

LEWIS: (*A momentary hesitation*) I want you to find someone for me.

ROBERT: Find someone?

LEWIS: Yes.

ROBERT: Lewis, don't you think you'd better tell me what this is all about?

LEWIS: Just over five years ago I sold my musical "Golden Girl", to Majestic Films. They bought it for Carol Spencer. You know what happened – Spencer died, and they didn't make it. Well, for some time now, ever since I've been in Hollywood in fact,I've been toying with the idea of buying the rights back from Majestic and ... well, making the project myself.

ROBERT: Go on, Lewis ...

LEWIS: About a month ago I met a man called John C. Reynolds. He was working with United Pictures, and he told me that a friend of his, an American millionaire called Rolf Winter, was interested in the movie business and wanted to start a company of his own. Winter was staying at the Mark Hopkins hotel in San Francisco and two weeks ago Reynolds and I flew down there to have a talk with him. Well, to cut a long story short, business-wise the trip was a fiasco. A complete bloody wash-out from start to finish.

ROBERT: What do you mean?

LEWIS: Not only was Winter not interested in the film business but it transpired that Reynolds hardly knew the guy. I was livid. I told Reynolds precisely what I thought of him, packed my bags, and was just about to return to Hollywood when to my surprise I received a phone call from Winter himself.

6

Fade in: phone ringing. Receiver is lifted.

LEWIS: (*On phone; impatiently*) Hello …

BETTY: Is that Mr Lewis Bristol?

LEWIS: Yes, it is …

BETTY: One moment, please. Mr Rolf Winter would like to speak to you.

WINTER: (*Pleasantly*) Hello? Mr Bristol? This is Rolf Winter. Mr Bristol, I think I owe you an apology. I was pretty rude to you yesterday afternoon, I guess.

LEWIS: Well, I must say, you didn't exactly endear yourself to me, Mr Winter.

WINTER: (*Amused*) No, I don't expect I did. Now don't get me wrong, Mr Bristol! I haven't changed my mind. I'm not going into the movie business. But I just wanted you to know that I've always enjoyed your music, Mr Bristol. It's always given me a great deal of pleasure.

LEWIS: (*Thawing*) Thank you.

WINTER: I saw "Golden Girl" three times. Twice in New York and once in London. A wonderful show.

LEWIS: Thank you, Mr Winter. It was kind of you to call.

WINTER: Are you returning to Hollywood today?

LEWIS: Yes, I'm flying back this morning.

WINTER: Oh, that sure is a pity. I was hoping you'd accept an invitation to my little party this evening.

LEWIS: Party?

WINTER: Yes. It's my birthday today. I'm fifty-eight. Come to think of it, that's a hell of a reason for giving a party!

LEWIS:	Well – happy birthday!
WINTER:	Thank you, sir. And if you change your mind and stay over, the party's at the Mark Hopkins. The Top of the Mark – from seven o'clock onwards.
LEWIS:	Thank you, Mr Winter. It's very kind of you.
WINTER:	I hope we shall have the pleasure of seeing you.
LEWIS:	Well – (*A sudden decision*) To hell with Hollywood! I need a break and I haven't seen San Francisco anyway. I'll be there, Mr Winter.
WINTER:	Why now, that's just fine! I'll look forward to seeing you, Mr Bristol. Oh – just one thing …
LEWIS:	Yes?
WINTER:	(*Start fade*) Don't bring Mr Reynolds.
LEWIS:	You needn't worry about that!

Complete fade.

LEWIS:	(*Fade in*) … I was staying at the Fairmont Hotel on Nob Hill; the Mark Hopkins is directly opposite and at about half past seven I strolled across the road and took the elevator up to The Top of the Mark.
ROBERT:	Top of the Mark?
LEWIS:	It's a sort of – well, a kind of penthouse. It's got fabulous views, right across San Francisco … When I arrived there was already about a hundred and fifty people there and the party was well under way. Winter spotted me immediately and I must say he was extremely friendly. It was a good party,

Robert, and I enjoyed it enormously. At about ten o'clock I decided to call it a day and was making my way towards Winter to say goodbye to him, when a girl jumped up from one of the tables. She was tall, with brown eyes and honey-coloured hair, and she was wearing a plain white dress. I wondered how the hell I'd missed her all evening. She was also carrying a glass of orange juice. At least she was – until she bumped into me.

Fade in: general chatter.
Background of small orchestra.

VIRGINIA: Oh!!!. Oh, my goodness! I'm terribly sorry – I do apologise, I ... Oh, just look at your shirt!

LEWIS: Don't worry, it's only orange juice.

VIRGINIA: <u>Only</u> orange juice! What on earth are you going to do?

LEWIS: I'll be home in two minutes – I'm staying at the Fairmont. There's absolutely nothing to worry about.

VIRGINIA: But I've ruined your evening?

LEWIS: No – no, I was leaving anyway.

VIRGINIA: I feel absolutely awful! I just don't know what to say.

LEWIS: Is your dress all right?

VIRGINIA: Yes. It all went on you, I'm afraid.

LEWIS: When you tell your friends about it, the name's Bristol, by the way. Lewis Bristol.

VIRGINIA: I'm – I'm awfully sorry, Mr Bristol. I really am – I do apologise.

LEWIS: You're English?

VIRGINIA: Yes. Does that make it all right?

LEWIS: (*Amused*) Do you live in San Francisco, or are you here on a visit?

VIRGINIA: No, I live here.

LEWIS: (*With a fairly aggressive friendliness*) Then you know the Fairmont. Meet me in the downstairs bar in half an hour. I'll buy you a dry martini.

VIRGINIA: I'm – I'm sorry, I'm afraid I don't drink.

LEWIS: Then I'll be brave and make it an orange juice.

VIRGINIA: (*Hesitating*) Well –

LEWIS: Considering you've spoilt my shirt and ruined my suit – to say nothing of this very English tie – that's the least you can do, Miss – er –

VIRGINIA: (*Suddenly*) All right. But you'd better make it forty-five minutes. I've only just arrived here.

LEWIS: (*Start Fade*) It's five past ten. Let's say eleven o'clock.

VIRGINIA: Eleven o'clock, Mr Bristol.

Complete Fade.

LEWIS: (*Fade in*) … She was late, nearly twenty minutes late, and I began to think she wasn't going to come. But she did, and after we'd both made the inevitable little jokes about orange juice she told me her name was Virginia Allen and that she worked for Rolf Winter. She was a lovely person, Robert – a really sweet girl – and I made up my mind there and then to stay in San Francisco and see a great deal more of her.

ROBERT: Good old Lewis! Still the fast worker – never misses a trick!

10

LEWIS:	(*Irritated; almost angry*) It wasn't like that! For God's sake, Robert! It wasn't a bit like that …
ROBERT:	(*Quietly*) Go on, Lewis …
LEWIS:	The next night I took her out to dinner, to a restaurant called Alioto's on Fisherman's Wharf. The following day, it was a Sunday, we hired a car and drove along the coast as far as Carmel. That was a wonderful day; I don't think I'll ever forget it. I didn't see her on the Monday because I had a cable from my office and I had to fly down to Los Angeles, but I was back in San Francisco on Tuesday night, and she met me at the airport. We had dinner together at a little restaurant on Nob Hill. (*A moment*) That was the night I asked her to marry me.

Fade in. background noises of tiny restaurant.

VIRGINIA:	Are you serious?
LEWIS:	Of course I'm serious.
VIRGINIA:	But – but we don't really know each other, Lewis. We only met last Friday, for the first time.
LEWIS:	What's that got to do with it? I'd known Eve for years – but it still didn't work out.
VIRGINIA:	(*After a moment*) Why didn't it work out, Lewis? What happened?
LEWIS:	Oh, I don't know … It's difficult to say. I was trying to write an operetta during the early days of our marriage and it wasn't going very well. I was edgy; moody, difficult to live with, and Eve just couldn't take it.
VIRGINIA:	What makes you think I can take it?

11

LEWIS:	I don't know whether you can. I'm just hoping you'll try.
VIRGINIA:	Well, I'll say one thing – you're honest, anyway.
LEWIS:	I don't want you to have any illusions about me, Virginia.
VIRGINIA:	But I've got to have illusions about you, Lewis, if I'm going to marry you! You can't marry a man if you've no illusions about him!
LEWIS:	(*Amused*) No, I suppose not.
SUKI:	(*Passing the table*) Hello, there!
VIRGINIA:	Oh, hello, Suki! How are you?
SUKI:	I'm fine! See you Thursday …
VIRGINIA:	(*To Lewis*) She's my hairdresser. She's from Honolulu. Don't you think she's cute? I love the way her eyes …
LEWIS:	(*Not listening to her*) Virginia – what do you say?
VIRGINIA:	(*A moment*) What happened to Eve, your wife? Is she still alive?
LEWIS:	Yes. She lives in London. She has a dress shop. La Boutique. It's in Marsham Mews, just off Sloane Street. I'm told she does very well with it.
VIRGINIA:	Do you ever see her?
LEWIS:	No – but then I'm hardly ever in London. I haven't been there for three years. My brother sees her; they're very good friends.
VIRGINIA:	Your brother? The one you told me about, at Scotland Yard?
LEWIS:	Yes. Robert. I've only got the one brother. I've a sister, Katherine. She's married to a Swiss. He runs a hotel in Venice.

12

VIRGINIA:	(*Trying to change the subject*) I've never been to Venice. It's a place I've always wanted to go to.
LEWIS:	Well, Virginia?
VIRGINIA:	(*Stalling*) Is Robert older than you?
LEWIS:	No, he's younger; quite a bit younger.
VIRGINIA:	And Katherine?
LEWIS:	(*Realising what she is doing*) Robert's thirty-seven. Katherine's thirty-three. And I shall be forty … five next November. Well, Virginia? What do you say?
VIRGINIA:	I've – I've never thought about marriage. Not seriously. I'm afraid I've always considered myself somewhat of a … (*Suddenly; almost nervously*) Lewis, do you think we could talk about this some other time?
LEWIS:	Does this mean the answer's no?
VIRGINIA:	No, no, it doesn't mean that at all! It's simply that … Look, come to my place tomorrow night. We'll talk about it then. I've an apartment in Mason House, that's on California Street near …
LEWIS:	I know the address. I picked you up on Sunday morning.
VIRGINIA:	Yes, of course you did! Apartment 24. Come along any time after seven.
LEWIS:	Virginia, I can't tell you – I can't begin to tell you – what these last five days have meant to me. If it'll help you to make up your mind, I'd like you to know that – there'll be no money problems, I'm quite well off. And we don't have to live in America, not if you don't want to.

13

VIRGINIA: (*Start Fade*) Lewis, can we talk about this tomorrow night? Please, darling ...

LEWIS: (*Puzzled*) Yes, of course. If that's what you want, Virginia.

Complete Fade.

LEWIS: (*Fade in*) ... I spent the next morning strolling round San Francisco and looking at my watch. I had lunch in the hotel and in the afternoon, out of desperation, I went to a movie. At seven o'clock, precisely, I was in the lobby of Mason House, waiting for the elevator to take me up to Virginia's apartment.

Sound of elevator. It stops. Door opens.

DONOVAN: (*Unmistakably Irish*) Good evening, sir.

LEWIS: Good evening. (*Entering elevator*) Apartment 24, please.

DONOVAN: (Surprised) Twenty-four, did you say?

LEWIS: Yes, Miss Allen.

DONOVAN: Miss – Allen?

LEWIS: (*Impatiently*) Yes; Miss Virginia Allen.

DONOVAN: I'm sorry, sir. There isn't a Miss Allen; not here. There's a Mr and Mrs Ballam in apartment 18, but they're in New York at the moment.

LEWIS: No, no, this is Miss Allen. Miss ... This <u>is</u> Mason House?

DONOVAN: Sure – this is Mason House, but you must have got the wrong address, sir. We haven't got an apartment 24. There are only eighteen apartments in the whole building.

14

LEWIS:	(*Puzzled*) But you're mistaken – surely. I met Miss Allen here, on Sunday morning. I picked her up. She was waiting … (*Stops*)
DONOVAN:	You picked her up – here, sir?
LEWIS:	(*Thoughtfully*) Yes; in the lobby, she was waiting for me.
DONOVAN:	Well, she may have been waiting for you in the lobby, sir, but the lady certainly doesn't live here. I've never heard of Miss Allen.
LEWIS:	Are you the janitor?
DONOVAN:	That's right. Donovan's the name. Ed Donovan. Been here seven years. I know all the tenants. They're friends of mine. Except the little bastard in Number 7.
LEWIS:	You say there's a Mr and Mrs Ballam in Number 18?
DONOVAN:	That's right.
LEWIS:	How old would Mrs Ballam be?
DONOVAN:	Oh – sixty-seven or eight. But she doesn't look it. She's a lulu. He's retired; used to be with General Motors.
LEWIS:	(*Thoughtfully*) Thank you, Donovan. (*Tipping him*) Here we are.
DONOVAN:	Oh, thank you sir. Sorry I can't be more helpful. (*Start Fade*) There's a list of the tenants on the wall over there, if you care to take a look at it …

Complete Fade.

LEWIS:	… I didn't waste time looking at the list; I knew, instinctively, that Donovan was telling the truth. I jumped in a cab and went round to the Mark Hopkins. Winter was in bed with a chill and had left orders not to be disturbed.

15

After a friendly argument with the Bell captain, I was eventually shown up to a suite on the fourteenth floor and introduced to a hatchet-faced woman called Betty Lane.

BETTY: (*Fade in*) ... I'm Betty Lane. Mr Winter's personal assistant. What can I do for you?

LEWIS: (*Friendly*) My name's Bristol – Lewis Bristol ...

BETTY: Yes, I know. What is it, Mr Bristol? What's on your mind?

LEWIS: Well – I was hoping Mr Winter might spare me a few minutes.

BETTY: That's impossible. Quite impossible. Mr Winter has a temperature and he's not seeing anyone. It's my guess he won't be seeing anyone for quite some time. Can I help you, Mr Bristol? But make it brief, please.

LEWIS: Miss Allen's a friend of mine, and I was going to ask Mr Winter if he'd be kind enough to give me ...

BETTY: Miss Allen? Who's Miss Allen?

LEWIS: Virginia Allen. She works for Mr Winter.

BETTY: (*Surprised*) She does?

LEWIS: Yes.

BETTY: This is news to me. What does Miss Allen do, exactly?

LEWIS: You mean – you've never heard of her?

BETTY: No, I'm afraid I haven't.

LEWIS: (*Hesitant*) Do you ... know most of the people who work for Mr Winter?

BETTY: I know all the people who work for Mr Winter. There's not many of us, anyway. (*With sarcasm*) Just the chosen few. Your friend's

16

	not on the payroll, Mr Bristol. I can assure you of that.
LEWIS:	(*Quietly*) I see.
BETTY:	Where did you meet this – Miss Allen?
LEWIS:	At the party.
BETTY:	Mr Winter's party?
LEWIS:	Yes.
BETTY:	And she told you she worked for him?
LEWIS:	(*Hesitant*) Er – yes, she did.
BETTY:	(*Amused*) It sounds to me as if you've been taken for a ride, Mr Bristol. (*Start Fade*) And I don't lean on the cable cars either …

Complete Fade.

LEWIS:	(*Fade in*) … When I arrived back at my hotel, I was told that a girl had phoned me at about half past eight but had refused to leave either a message or her name. Whether it was Virginia or not, I don't know.
ROBERT:	Go on, Lewis …
LEWIS:	The next day I returned to Mason House and had another talk to Donovan. He stuck to his story, of course, and to substantiate it even introduced me to two of the tenants. They'd never heard of Virginia. For three days – for three whole days, Robert – I walked around San Francisco in the hope of finding her. I went to restaurants, cafés, places we'd visited together …
ROBERT:	(*Interrupting*) But what about her friends? Surely you'd met some of her friends?
LEWIS:	No; no, I hadn't. As a matter of fact, it gradually dawned on me that although I was in love with the girl, I really knew very little

17

	about her. We'd seen a great deal of each other, of course, but – (*Hesitates*) I'm afraid I'd always done the talking. And about myself, as usual.
ROBERT:	(*Quietly*) Go on …
LEWIS:	On the third day, just when I was feeling pretty desperate, I suddenly remembered the girl Virginia had spoken to in the restaurant on Nob Hill.
ROBERT:	The hairdresser?
LEWIS:	That's right. I remembered that Virginia had called her Suki and for the first time I really felt I had something to go on. I went down to the hairdressing salon in the hotel and had a chat to the receptionist. She was a coloured girl and a real sweetie and although she'd never heard of Virginia, she said she'd find Suki for me if she had to call every beauty establishment in San Francisco. Late that afternoon she phoned me. She said Suki's name was Talmadge – Suki Talmadge – and that she worked for a beauty specialist called André Marquand.
ROBERT:	He wouldn't be French, by any chance?
LEWIS:	Yes, he was French all right. More French than the French, if you ask me. On the Monday morning I went round to Marquand's establishment and told him, quite frankly, that I was trying to find a client of his called Virginia Allen. I said I'd been searching for her for several days and I'd be most grateful for any help he could give me. (*A moment*) I don't have to tell you what happened. He'd never heard of Virginia.

18

ROBERT: And the girl – Suki?

LEWIS: (*Start Fade*) I questioned him about Suki and he said …

Complete Fade.

ANDRE: (*Fade In*) … I'm sorry, Miss Talmadge – Suki – doesn't work here any longer. She left, two days ago.

LEWIS: What do you mean?

ANDRE: What I say. She left me; two days ago. (*Puzzled*) Don't ask me to explain, I don't understand it myself. We'd been good friends; very good friends for almost four years. Then on Saturday morning she came in and she said, "Monsieur André, I'm sorry – I'm very sorry, but I'm leaving you." And she left – just like that.

LEWIS: Well – where's she gone? Do you know?

ANDRE: No, I don't. She told one of the girls that she was going to work at the Hilton in New York, but I don't know whether that's true or not. (*Suddenly*) Look, I'm sorry – you'll have to excuse me. I'm very, very busy this morning.

LEWIS: (*His thoughts elsewhere*) Yes, of course. I'm sorry to have troubled you.

ANDRE: No, no, please – I only wish I could help you. (*Curious*) You say … you've been looking for this girl for several days?

LEWIS: Yes.

ANDRE: Well, why don't you hire a detective, Mr Bristol?

LEWIS: A detective?

ANDRE: Yes; a private-eye. Let him try and find this friend of yours.

LEWIS: (*Start Fade*) That's not a bad idea. (*Impressed*) Not at all a bad idea. Thank you, Mr Marquand …

Complete Fade.

ROBERT: (*Fade in*) ... And did you hire yourself a
...private-eye?

LEWIS: Yes, I did. I made a few enquiries and eventually
went to see a man called Dave Dyce.

ROBERT: Dave Dyce. He sounds like a character out of
"Guys and Dolls".

LEWIS: Yes, I know, but he wasn't a bit like that. He was
tall and effeminate, and he has a phoney English
accent. I told him about Virginia; I told him
exactly what had happened, and he said he didn't
think there was any doubt that he'd be able to find
her for me. He also said he didn't want to be
tiresome, but his fee was three thousand dollars,
in advance.

ROBERT: Good God, it takes me months to earn that sort of
money! Go on, Lewis. What happened?

LEWIS: The bastard didn't find her. He didn't even try.

ROBERT: What do you mean?

LEWIS: Twenty-four hours after our interview he sent my
cheque back, together with a copy of the New
York Times. He said he was sorry, but the case no
longer interested him.

ROBERT: Yes, but – why the New York Times?

LEWIS: That puzzled me at first. I couldn't understand it.
Then I found a new item, tucked away in the stop
press. The body of a girl had been found in
Central Park. She'd been murdered; stabbed to
death. (*A moment*) It was Suki.

ROBERT: Suki Talmadge?

LEWIS: Yes.

ROBERT: (*Intrigued*) Go on, Lewis.

LEWIS: That's it. That's the whole story. I stayed in San Francisco until the end of the week, hoping that Virginia would contact me. But she didn't. On the Sunday night I flew back to Hollywood.

ROBERT: And you never saw or heard from her again?

LEWIS: No, I didn't.

ROBERT: (*After a momentary hesitation*) Well, I dare say there's a perfectly simple explanation for all this.

LEWIS: If there is, I'd like to know what it is.

ROBERT: Lewis, tell me: did you buy this girl anything? Furs – jewellery …

LEWIS: No – and I didn't lend her any money either, if that's what you're thinking. (*Suddenly; urgently*) Now I'll tell you why I really sent you that cable, Robert. I'll tell you exactly what I want you to do for me. I want you to cancel your Italian trip and fly out to San Francisco. I'll pay all expenses, of course, and give you …

ROBERT: (*Stopping him*) Lewis, for heaven's sake! I can't fly out to California, not at a moment's notice.

LEWIS: (*Surprised*) Why not? You're on leave. You told me yourself you don't have to be back in the office for three weeks.

ROBERT: Yes, but – (*Laughing*) I don't want to go to America! I want to go to Venice. I want to see Katherine. Besides, don't be ridiculous, I'd never find this girl! Not in a thousand years. Now my advice to you …

LEWIS: I don't want your advice! I want your help.

ROBERT: Lewis, I know how you feel. I know exactly how …

LEWIS: (*Annoyed*) You don't know how I feel! I was in love with Virginia. Desperately in love with her. I still am.

21

ROBERT: (*Quietly*) You were in love with Eve once, remember …

LEWIS: What the hell's that got to do with it?

ROBERT: … And the little girl you took to the South of France. To say nothing of the voluptuous Norwegian that couldn't speak a word of English   …

LEWIS: Robert, you just haven't heard a word I've said! You simply haven't been listening to me for the past fifteen minutes! This wasn't like that! This wasn't an affair – this was quite different!

ROBERT: You mean: this time she walked out on you, instead of you walking out on her?

LEWIS: Oh, for God's sake!

ROBERT: I'm sorry, Lewis. I can't help you.

LEWIS: (*Angry, but managing to control himself*) All right. Well – that's that. There's nothing more to be said. Would you like another drink?

ROBERT: No, thank you …

LEWIS: When are you leaving for Italy?

ROBERT: I'm flying to Rome tomorrow morning. I shall probably stay there two or three days before going on to Venice.

LEWIS: Well – give my love to Katherine and Freddie when you see them.

ROBERT: Yes, of course. Good Lord, is it ten o'clock? I must be making a move.

LEWIS: Wait a moment! (*A moment*) I'm sorry I lost my temper just now…

ROBERT: Forget it.

LEWIS: But if you won't help me, then at least …

ROBERT: (*Good natured*) What do you mean – won't help you? For goodness' sake be serious,

22

Lewis! I'm a Scotland Yard man; I can't fly out to the States at a moment's notice! And even if I could – how could I possibly find this girl? It'd be like looking for a needle in a haystack.

LEWIS: All right, Robert. All right, dear boy, you've made your point. But at least – tell me what you think about all this. (*Puzzled and genuinely concerned*) What happened, Robert? What went wrong? Did she just … walk out on me?

ROBERT: (*A moment; then frankly*) I don't know.

LEWIS: And why did she lie to me about – well, about the apartment and working for Rolf Winter? And the murder, Robert? Suki Talmadge. Was that anything to do with Virginia – was that connected in some way with her disappearance?

ROBERT: (*Quietly*) I don't know, Lewis.

Fade In Music.

Fade Music.
Door opens.

MRS WEBB: Now are you sure you've got everything, sir? Have you got the two sports shirts that came back from the laundry?

ROBERT: Yes, I've got the lot! Now don't worry about a thing while I'm away, Mrs Webb. Just take care of yourself.

MRS WEBB: Yes, and you take care of yourself, Mr Bristol, and don't forget to give your sister and her husband my very kind … (*A sudden thought*) Oh, my goodness!

ROBERT: What is it?

MRS WEBB:	Here am I telling you not to forget anything, and I've forgotten something myself! (*Opens a drawer*) Mrs Bristol sent this belt round yesterday afternoon, sir. She said you knew all about it.
ROBERT:	Oh, yes! It's for Katherine. My sister bought a dress from Mrs Bristol the last time she was over here, then lost the belt. Eve's been trying to get her another one ever since. Give it to me, I'll put it in my suitcase.

Phone rings.

ROBERT:	It's all right, Mrs Webb. I'll answer it. (*Lifts receiver*) Kensington 8271 …
EVE:	(*On the other end*) Robert? This is Eve …
ROBERT:	Hello, Eve!
EVE:	I've just rung up to say – have a nice holiday.
ROBERT:	Thank you, my dear.
EVE:	Did Mrs Webb give you the belt?
ROBERT:	Yes, I've got it. Don't worry, I'll see Katherine gets it all right.
EVE:	Thank you, Robert. Have a good time – and give my love to Katherine and Freddie.
ROBERT:	Yes, of course.
EVE:	(*A shade too casual*) Oh, by the way – I suppose you know Lewis is over here?
ROBERT:	Yes. How did you know, Eve?
EVE:	(*Faintly embarrassed*) There – there was a picture of him in the paper this morning. Have you seen him, Robert?
ROBERT:	Yes; we had a drink together last night.
EVE:	How is he?
ROBERT:	Oh – much the same. You know Lewis.
EVE:	Is – is he alone?
ROBERT:	Yes, he's alone.

24

EVE:	How long is he staying over here?
ROBERT:	I think he said a week, but I'm not sure. Look, Eve – I'll drop in the shop on the way to the airport and give you all the news.
EVE:	Have you got time?
ROBERT:	Yes, I've got bags of time.
EVE:	(*Pleased*) All right, Robert – do that.
ROBERT:	See you in about twenty minutes.
EVE:	Lucky you! I wish I was going to Venice.
ROBERT:	Eve, who are you kiddin'? Right now you'd sooner be in London than anywhere else in the world – and you know it.
EVE:	Well ... Don't be long, darling – then we can go out and have a coffee.

Fade in Music.
Slow Fade.

Cross-Fade Music into sound of motor launch on Grand Canal, Venice. Launch arrives at hotel landing stage. Background of excited voices.

MARIO:	Let me help you, Signora.
KATHERINE:	Thank you, Mario. Has my brother arrived?
MARIO:	Just five minutes ago. Please – give me your parcels, Signora. I'll take care of them.
FREDDIE:	(*Approaching*) Hello, Katherine!
KATHERINE:	Hello, darling! Robert's arrived then?
FREDDIE:	Yes; I've just taken him up to his room. He's delighted with it. (*Suddenly*) There he is now! He's on the balcony!
KATHERINE:	(*Calling*) Robert!
ROBERT:	(*Calling from the balcony*) Hello, Katherine!
KATHERINE:	(Calling) I'll be with you in two minutes!
FREDDIE:	(*Start Fade*) Mario, Mrs Rafino has booked a table for this evening – for six people, at eight

25

o'clock. She wants to speak to you about the menu.

Complete Fade.

A door opens.

ROBERT: Katherine! How wonderful to see you again!

KATHERINE: (*Kissing him*) Robert, darling, I'm sorry I couldn't meet you at the station. A friend of mine was rushed into hospital last night and …

ROBERT: Katherine, don't be silly! Let me take a good look at you. You look wonderful! Not a day over twenty-eight.

KATHERINE: What do you mean? I am twenty-eight! I've been twenty-eight for five years! You look very well, Robert.

ROBERT: I am well.

KATHERINE: Did you enjoy Rome?

ROBERT: Enormously. I was only there three days but it was very exciting.

KATHERINE: How's things at home? How's Mrs Webb?

ROBERT: Oh, she's fine; she sends her love. And so does Eve, of course. Oh, by the way, I'm terribly sorry, Katherine! You know that belt, the one that Eve asked me to …

KATHERINE: Now don't tell me you've forgotten it!

ROBERT: Yes – I must have done. It's not here. (*Puzzled*) But I don't understand it! I'm damned if I understand it! I put it in this case myself, I'm absolutely sure I did.

KATHERINE: (*Laughing at him*) I know what you did – you left it on the bed!

ROBERT: No, I didn't, Katherine!

26

KATHERINE: Don't worry, it's not important. I'll drop Mrs Webb a card, she'll send it on. Tell me: how is Eve? Is she well?

ROBERT: Yes, she's fine and she's doing extremely well with "La Boutique". A great deal better than any of us expected.

KATHERINE: Well, let's face it – we thought she'd go bust. Is she on holiday at the moment?

ROBERT: No, I don't think so. In fact, I'm sure she isn't. (*Puzzled*) Why? What made you think she was on holiday?

KATHERINE: Well, a rather curious thing happened yesterday afternoon. I thought I saw her.

ROBERT: Eve?

KATHERINE: Yes.

ROBERT: Here in Venice?

KATHERINE: Yes.

ROBERT: But Eve wouldn't come to Venice, not without getting in touch with you and Freddie.

KATHERINE: No; of course she wouldn't. But it was terribly like her.

ROBERT: Yes, well it wasn't her, I can assure you. Wild horses wouldn't drag Eve away from London at the moment.

KATHERINE: Why do you say that?

ROBERT: Lewis is at the Savoy. He arrived on Tuesday.

KATHERINE: Lewis! But I thought he was in the States? He wrote me a long letter about ... Have you seen him?

ROBERT: Yes, I had a drink with him the night before I left.

KATHERINE: Was he – alone?

ROBERT: (*Laughing*) You and Eve! You always ask the same questions.

KATHERINE: No, I'm serious, Robert. I've a reason for asking. He wrote me a long letter, from San Francisco. He said he'd met an English girl over there and he was crazy about her and they were going to get married.

ROBERT: Yes, well – they didn't get married. She walked out on him.

KATHERINE: (*Stunned*) Walked out on him!

ROBERT: Yes.

KATHERINE: You mean a girl actually had the audacity, the impertinence, the sheer gall to walk out on our own, dear, unselfish little Lewis.

ROBERT: Yes.

KATHERINE: I don't believe it! I just don't believe it!

ROBERT: It's true, Katherine.

KATHERINE: (*Bursting with curiosity*) But what happened? Tell me about it, Robert!

ROBERT: Well – several weeks ago Lewis flew down to San Francisco to see an American millionaire called … Look, it's a long story, Katherine, and I'm just dying to get out of these clothes and take a shower. (*Start Fade*) I'll tell you and Freddie all about it at dinner…

Complete Fade.

Fade in: background noises of terrace restaurant on the Grand Canal. Distant sound of music.

KATHERINE: … But it's an incredible story, Robert! I can hardly believe it! You mean – she didn't phone him, or write him a letter, or …?

ROBERT: He never heard a word from her.

KATHERINE: But – what happened?

ROBERT: Nothing. He stayed in San Francisco until the weekend then flew back to Hollywood.

KATHERINE: Well, I don't often feel sorry for Lewis, but I must say, it sounds as if he's had a pretty raw deal. Freddie, what do you make of all this?

FREDDIE: I don't know what to make of it. Life's full of surprises.

ROBERT: (*Laughing*) That's a very profound statement, Freddie.

KATHERINE: Yes, and knowing Freddie it means he hasn't listened to a word you've said!

FREDDIE: Nonsense, Katherine!

KATHERINE: It's true! I've been watching you, darling. You've been miles away, thinking about the hotel the whole time.

FREDDIE: (*Unruffled*) Don't listen to her, Robert. I've heard every word; every single word you've said.

KATHERINE: Then what did you mean – life's full of surprises?

FREDDIE: I'll tell you what I meant, Katherine. This nan – the man Lewis met. Rolf Winter. He's here, in Venice.

KATHERINE: (*Astonished*) Are you sure, Freddie?

FREDDIE: Yes. As a matter of fact, you've seen him, Katherine. He was here the night before last – on the very next table – having dinner with his daughter.

KATHERINE: The big man, with grey hair – he complained about everything?

FREDDIE: That's right.

KATHERINE: Are you sure that was Winter?

29

FREDDIE:	Yes, I'm quite sure. (*Turning*) Mario, that man who sat on the next table on the night before last. The American ...
MARIO:	Mr Winter?
FREDDIE:	Yes. Did you say he was staying at the Gritti Palace?
MARIO:	I think so, sir. In fact I'm sure he is.
ROBERT:	Is that Mr Rolf Winter?
MARIO:	Yes, sir. Mr Rolf Winter. A very difficult gentleman.
KATHERINE:	Yes, he was complaining about something the other night.
MARIO:	The orange juice, Signora – and he wasn't even drinking it! I don't know how his poor wife stands it!
FREDDIE:	His wife? I thought ...
KATHERINE:	Surely that's not his wife – the good-looking girl he was having dinner with?
MARIO:	Yes, that's Mrs Winter.
FREDDIE:	I'm surprised. I thought it was his daughter.
MARIO:	No, sir, it's his wife. They've only been married about ten days. She's English, of course.
ROBERT:	English?
MARIO:	Yes, sir.
ROBERT:	(*Curious*) You don't happen to know her name, Mario? I mean – what her husband calls her?
MARIO:	No, I'm afraid I ... wait a moment! Yes ... Virginia. (*Amused*) "Virginia, honey", he calls her.
ROBERT:	(*Quietly*) Thank you, Mario.
MARIO:	Is everything all right, Mr Bristol? You've enjoyed your dinner?

ROBERT: Yes, very much, thank you.

KATHERINE: (*Quickly*) Is this the same girl? Is this the girl that Lewis was friendly with?

ROBERT: (*Thoughtfully*) Well, it's the same name …

KATHERINE: And she's English …

ROBERT: Yes.

FREDDIE: Surely … it must be the same girl.

KATHERINE: It must be, Robert!

Fade in Music.

Fade Music.

Fade in: distance background of noises and music of Piazza San Marco.

ROBERT: How long will it take us from here, Katherine?

KATHERINE: About ten minutes, that's all. Robert, what are you going to do when we get to the Gritti?

ROBERT: I'm going to ask for Mr Winter.

KATHERINE: Yes, I know, but – then what?

ROBERT: I shall tell Winter that my brother told me to look him up.

KATHERINE: And then?

ROBERT: It's nearly lunch-time. I suggest we all have a drink together.

KATHERINE: (*Quietly*) I see …

ROBERT: What's the matter, Katherine? You sound nervous.

KATHERINE: Well – yes, I am.

ROBERT: But this was your idea. You said – let's take a closer look at Mrs Winter. Let's try and find out if she really is the same person.

KATHERINE: Yes, I know – but –

ROBERT: You've changed your mind?

31

KATHERINE: No, I haven't changed my mind, but – I can't help wondering if Lewis really told you the truth about what happened in San Francisco.

ROBERT: I've no illusions about Lewis, I don't think either of us have. (*Start Fade*) But he told me the truth, Katherine. I'm sure of that.

Complete Fade.

Fade in : voice of Luigi.

LUIGI: (*On phone*) This is the Concierge speaking … I think you must have the wrong number, sir, this is the Gritti Palace … No, no, you want San Marco 2774 … Thank you, sir. (*Replaces receiver*) Good afternoon …

ROBERT: Good afternoon. I'd like to have a word with Mr Winter. I understand he and his wife are staying here.

LUIGI: Mr Rolf Winter?

ROBERT: Yes.

LUIGI: I'm sorry, sir. Mr and Mrs Winter left for London yesterday morning.

ROBERT: Oh – you don't happen to know where they're staying in London, by any chance?

LUIGI: I understand they're staying at Claridge's, sir.

ROBERT: Thank you.

LUIGI: Thank you, sir.

ROBERT: Well – that's that, Katherine. I don't see what else we can do.

KATHERINE: Except write to Lewis.

ROBERT: And tell him what? That his girlfriend – if it is his girlfriend – has suddenly turned up, and she's now married to a millionaire.

KATHERINE: I see what you mean. We'd better think about it …

ROBERT: (*Start Fade*) Over a large dry martini in Harry's Bar.

KATHERINE: (*Laughing*) Yes, all right, Robert.

Complete Fade.

MARIO: (*Fade in*) Good morning, Mr Bristol! Would you like some more coffee, sir?

ROBERT: No, thank you, Mario. (*Relaxed*) My goodness, it's a lovely day. I shall think about this when I'm back in London. Sunshine. Breakfast on the terrace.

MARIO: You should have been here last November, sir.

KATHERINE: Good morning, Robert. Have you had breakfast?

ROBERT: I'm just finishing.

KATHERINE: There's a letter for you, from London.

ROBERT: Thank you. (*Takes letter and opens it.*)

MARIO: Will you be in for lunch, madam?

KATHERINE: No, Mr Hauptmann's having the day off, for a change. We're all going to the Lido.

ROBERT: Katherine …

KATHERINE: Yes?

ROBERT: This isn't a letter … It's just a photograph … (*A moment; puzzled*) Why it's … La Boutique!

Fade in Music.

Fade down Music.

Fade in: typewriter. Door opens.

HILDA: Good morning, Inspector …

DALY: (*Urgently*) Hilda, get Continentals and tell them I want a call to Venice. The number's – wait a minute. I've got it here somewhere …

33

	Oh, here we are. San Marco 2986. Hotel Cristallo. A personal call to Robert Bristol.
HILDA:	Yes, sir.
DALY:	I'll be in my office. I don't want any other calls and I don't want to see anyone, not until I've spoken to the Superintendent.
HILDA:	(*Puzzled*) Very good, sir. You look worried, Inspector.
DALY:	You can say that again, Hilda! How in God's name do you tell a colleague – and a good friend into the bargain – that his brother's just been murdered?
HILDA:	His brother? You mean – Lewis Bristol, the composer?
DALY:	Yes.
HILDA:	He's been murdered?
DALY:	Yes; he was found early this morning in a shop called La Boutique.
HILDA:	La Boutique?
DALY:	It's a dress shop in Marsham Mews; belongs to his ex-wife.
HILDA:	(*Astonished*) But – But what happened?
DALY:	We don't know what happened. We don't even know what he was doing in the shop. All we know is he was sprawled across a chair – with a knife in his back.

Door opens.

EDWARDS:	Excuse me, sir.
DALY:	Hello, Sergeant! What are you doing here? I told you to stay at the shop.
EDWARDS:	Yes, I know, sir, but – do you think I could have a word with you, Inspector?
DALY:	(*After a moment*) Yes, come into the office. Get me that call, Hilda!

Door opens.

DALY: (*Closing door*) Well – what is it?

EDWARDS: I've got something in this case I'd like you to take a look at, sir. (*Opens case*) It's a belt – off a dress.

DALY: (*Faintly irritated*) Yes, I can see what it is, Sergeant.

EDWARDS: I've shown it to Mrs Bristol and she's very puzzled, sir. She says she gave this belt – this particular belt – to the Superintendent.

DALY: To the Superintendent?

EDWARDS: Yes, sir. She's adamant about it. Apparently, the Superintendent's sister bought a dress from La Boutique the last time she was over here and …

DALY: (*Interrupting him; impatient*) Look, Sergeant – what is this? What are you getting at? Where did you find this belt?

EDWARDS: It was on the dead man, sir.

Fade in Music.

Fade Music.

End of Part One

Part Two

Announcements. Music.
Fade Music.

EDWARDS: I've got something in this case I'd like you to take a look at, sir. (*Opens case*) It's a belt – off a dress.

DALY: (*Faintly irritated*) Yes, I can see what it is, Sergeant.

EDWARDS: I've shown it to Mrs Bristol and she's very puzzled, sir. She says she gave this belt – this particular belt – to the Superintendent.

DALY: To the Superintendent?

EDWARDS: Yes, sir. She's adamant about it. Apparently, the Superintendent's sister bought a dress from La Boutique the last time she was over here and …

DALY: (*Interrupting him; impatient*) Look, Sergeant – what is this? What are you getting at? Where did you find this belt?

EDWARDS: It was on the dead man, sir.

DALY: What do you mean <u>on</u> the dead man?

EDWARDS: It was in his coat pocket, sir.

DALY: (*After a moment; puzzled*) All right, Edwards. Leave it with me. Who's at La Boutique?

EDWARDS: Thornton and Hale, sir. They should be finished by eleven o'clock. Although it looks as if Thornton's going to run into a spot of trouble.

DALY: What kind of trouble?

EDWARDS: Miss Mortimer refused to have her fingerprints taken.

DALY: But it was Miss Mortimer that discovered the body!

EDWARDS: Yes, I know, sir.

Buzzer sounds.

DALY: (*Annoyed*) Then what the devil is she talking about? Look, if that woman refuses to cooperate then … (*Flicking down switch as buzzer sounds again*) What is it, Hilda?

HILDA: (*On speaker*) We're through to Venice, sir – Superintendent Bristol's on the line.

DALY: Thank you. (*Lifts receiver*) Hello? (*A pause*) Hello? …

ROBERT: (*On the other end*) Robert Bristol speaking …

DALY: Robert, this is Daly. Eric Daly.

ROBERT: (*Surprised*) Hello, Eric! I wondered who the devil it was! What's happened?

DALY: Robert, listen. I've got some bad news for you. Very bad news, I'm afraid. Lewis … your brother … (*Hesitates*)

ROBERT: (*Puzzled*) What about Lewis?

DALY: He's been murdered …

Fade in Music.

Fade Music.
Robert in telephone box. Number being dialled.
Number ringing out.

PEARL: (*On the other end; a faintly masculine voice*) La Boutique …

Quick pips. Coin inserted.

ROBERT: Is that Miss Mortimer?

PEARL: Yes, speaking …

ROBERT: Can I speak with Eve, please? This is Robert Bristol.

PEARL: (*Quickly*) Oh, one moment, Mr Bristol!

A slight pause.

EVE: (*Tensely; on phone*) Robert, where are you? Have you heard about … Lewis? …

ROBERT: Yes, I've heard.

EVE: Where are you speaking from?

ROBERT: I'm at London Airport. I've just arrived. Eve, listen – I'm going straight to the Yard and then I'll pick you up at the shop. I want to talk to you.

EVE: Yes, of course. Are you alone?

ROBERT: Yes; Katherine's flying over tomorrow. I'll try to be at La Boutique by five o'clock but it may be a little later.

EVE: I'll wait for you! It doesn't matter what time it is, I'll be here!

ROBERT: (*Concerned for her*) Are you all right, Eve?

EVE: Yes, but – it's been terrible, Robert.

ROBERT: I'm sure it has.

EVE: It was such a shock, I … I don't even know what Lewis was doing here.

ROBERT: Did you discover the … Did you find him?

EVE: No. Pearl did. She arrived early this morning. She had some work to do on the accounts and … (*Distressed*) Oh, God, it was awful! I wouldn't like to live through this morning again.

ROBERT: Don't worry, my dear. I'll take care of everything.

EVE: I'm – I'm glad you're back, Robert.

ROBERT: I'll see you later, Eve.

Robert replaces receiver and opens the door of telephone box. Background noises.

Fade noises.

DALY: (*Fade in*) … Miss Mortimer arrived at the shop at about half past eight. She didn't see Lewis at first, he'd been dumped in a chair and someone – the murderer presumably – had covered the body with a couple of dresses.

ROBERT: How long had the body been there?

41

DALY: We don't know. According to the doctor he'd
           been dead about six hours. But remember, he may
           not have been murdered at La Boutique, the body
           could have been taken there after the murder was
           committed.

ROBERT: Do you think it was taken there? Do you think
           that's what happened?

DALY: I don't know. If it was, then the murderer – or an
           accomplice at any rate – had a key. There was no
           sign of the shop being broken into.

ROBERT: How many keys are there?

DALY: Two. Miss Mortimer has one and Mrs Bristol, of
           course. (*A moment*) Robert, tell me: what sort of
           a woman is Miss Mortimer?

ROBERT: You've seen her. Tough; capable; very difficult
           sometimes.

DALY: Yes, I realise that. But what's her background –
           where does she come from?

ROBERT: I don't know her very well. When Eve – Mrs
           Bristol – first started La Boutique, she ran into
           financial difficulties. Miss Mortimer lent her
           some money and then, more or less for
           something to do I gather, started to take an
           interest in the business.

DALY: Are they partners?

ROBERT: Well – I don't know what their financial
           arrangements are, but – yes, I should say they
           were more or less partners.

DALY: Was Miss Mortimer in business for herself,
           originally?

ROBERT: No, she was a school-teacher. Her father was in
           the Consular service. She's lived all over the
           place. Vienna, Mexico City, New Orleans …

42

She's a damned interesting woman, if she wasn't so bad-tempered all the time.

DALY: Well – in spite of her temper she and Mrs Bristol must get on well together.

ROBERT: They do; they get on like a house on fire. Which amazes me, because on the very few occasions I've met Miss Mortimer she'd rubbed me up the wrong way in next to no time.

DALY: Yes, I can believe it. Even Thornton's having trouble with her – she refuses to have her fingerprints taken. And let's face it, Rod Thornton doesn't usually have trouble with the opposite sex. (*A moment*) Robert, do you mind if I ask you a few ... personal ... questions about Mrs Bristol?

ROBERT: Of course not. Go ahead.

DALY: (*Stalling*) She's a very nice woman, a charming woman, in fact, and I'm sure that ...

ROBERT: Ask the questions, Eric.

DALY: How friendly was she with your brother?

ROBERT: Friendly? They were divorced.

DALY: Yes, I know they were divorced, but when I questioned her, I got the impression that in spite of the divorce she was still very fond of him.

ROBERT: She's always been fond of Lewis.

DALY: Then why did she tell me that she hadn't seen him for several years; that she didn't even know he was in London?

ROBERT: Did she tell you that?

DALY: Yes.

ROBERT: Well – it's probably true. After all, he spent most of his time in America.

DALY: But during the past week, while he's been staying at the Savoy, there's been several newspaper articles about him. He was even on a television

43

programme. I find it just a little difficult to believe that she didn't know he was over here.

ROBERT: (*After a moment*) Yes, I agree. Leave Eve – Mrs Bristol – to me, Eric. I'll have a talk to her.

DALY: Thank you. I was hoping you'd say that. Now I wonder if you'd give me a few details about Lewis. How old was he, Robert?

ROBERT: Forty-eight. No, wait a minute. Yes; forty-eight.

DALY: Was he a wealthy man?

ROBERT: God knows! I haven't a clue. He earned a lot, of course – a great deal – but he was a tremendous spender. I shall be very surprised if he's left a lot of money.

DALY: If he has, then who do you think he's left it to?

ROBERT: Eric, I just wouldn't know! Your guess is as good as mine.

DALY: Robert, just before you went on holiday your brother sent you a cable asking you to meet him at the Savoy.

ROBERT: That's right.

DALY: Did you meet him?

ROBERT: Yes, I did.

DALY: Did he seem perfectly normal? Was he in good spirits?

ROBERT: No; he was worried about a girl he'd met in San Francisco. He said he'd fallen in love with her and, not to put too fine a point on it, she'd walked out on him – disappeared, in fact. He asked me to go out to California and try to find her.

DALY: And what did you say?

ROBERT: What do you think I said? I told him not to be a damn fool. (*A moment*) Poor Lewis … He really did go overboard for people.

44

DALY: What was the name of this girl? Was it Allen – Virginia Allen?

ROBERT: (*Surprised*) Why, yes …

DALY: We found a diary on Lewis; her name was written in it. Several times, as a matter of fact. (*Hesitates, then:*) Robert, tell me: did Mrs Bristol give you a belt, off a dress, and ask you to take it to Venice for her?

ROBERT: (*Puzzled*) Yes, she did. My sister Katherine, who lives in Venice, bought a dress from La Boutique some time ago and unfortunately lost … But how do you know about the belt?

DALY: (*Ignoring the question*) Did you take it to Venice?

ROBERT: No, I didn't. I forgot it, as a matter of fact.

DALY: And left it behind?

ROBERT: Yes.

DALY: Where?

ROBERT: (*Still puzzled*) Well – I left it at my flat, I imagine. It certainly wasn't in my case when I … But, look – Eric, what is this?

DALY: Your brother was wearing an overcoat; we found the belt in one of the pockets.

ROBERT: I – I don't believe this!

DALY: It's true.

ROBERT: But how did he get hold of it?

DALY: We don't know, Robert.

ROBERT: Are you sure it's the same belt?

DALY: Mrs Bristol says it is. (*Drawer opens*) But you take a look at it: let's hear what you think. Here it is. (*A pause*) Well?

ROBERT: Yes; it certainly looks like the same belt. Has O'Hara examined it?

DALY: Yes; he's examined the belt and the buckle. There's nothing unusual about them. It's just an ordinary belt off a silk dress.

ROBERT: (*Bewildered; almost angry*) Then what the hell was it doing in Lewis's pocket?

Fade in Music.

Fade Music.

Sound of shop door opening; closing.

PEARL: (*On phone; in background*) ... But surely you said you were going to collect the coat, madam ... I'm quite sure you did ... No, I'm sorry, Mrs Bristol isn't here at the moment ... No, no, there's no need to do that, I'll jump in a cab and bring it round myself ... Not at all, madam. (*Replaces receiver*)

ROBERT: Good evening, Miss Mortimer.

PEARL: Oh, hello, Mr Bristol!

ROBERT: Is Eve about?

PEARL: She's just slipped out to the chemist's, she'll be back in a moment.

ROBERT: Is she all right?

PEARL: Yes, but we've both had the most ghastly headaches all day.

ROBERT: I'm not surprised. It must have been a terrible shock for you, finding Lewis like that.

PEARL: My God, it was! The extraordinary thing is I didn't believe it. I thought I was seeing things at first ... I picked up two dresses ... I don't know why, I was just pottering about ... and there he was with the knife sticking out of his back.

ROBERT: You've no idea what my brother was doing here?

PEARL: Haven't the slightest idea. He certainly didn't come to see me, or Eve either for that matter.

46

ROBERT: Did you know Lewis? Had you met him?

PEARL: No; I'd never seen him before. But I recognised him immediately from the photograph …

ROBERT: Which photograph?

PEARL: Eve has a photograph of him; she keeps it in a drawer in her desk.

ROBERT: (*Quietly*) I see.

PEARL: (*Abruptly*) Your brother was a bit of a womaniser, wasn't he?

ROBERT: (*Irritated*) He had his faults. Who hasn't?

PEARL: Yes, I know, but didn't he ditch Eve and go off with someone else?

ROBERT: No, not exactly; he just left her and went to America. Miss Mortimer, tell me …

PEARL: Pearl, please! I had the "Miss Mortimer" treatment this morning, for five whole hours.

ROBERT: Tell me: why did you refuse to have your fingerprints taken?

PEARL: Because the little squirt of a Sergeant was too full of himself. He didn't ask me – he simply told me he was going to take them! I don't take kindly to being told to do things, Mr Bristol. Except by Eve, of course. I'd do anything for poor old Eve!

ROBERT: Poor old Eve … You sound as if you're sorry for her.

PEARL: No, I'm not sorry for her, I … As a matter of fact I'm very worried about her. I have been for several days.

ROBERT: Why?

PEARL: I don't know why. It's just that I have an uneasy feeling that she's in trouble of some kind.

ROBERT: Has she told you that she's in trouble?

PEARL: (*A note of tenseness in her voice*) No, no, she hasn't.

ROBERT: Then why should you think that …

PEARL: Look, can we talk about this some other time? She may walk in at any minute, and I should hate her to think that we were talking about her behind her back.

ROBERT: (*Quietly; yet with authority*) If she walks in then we'll stop talking about her. Now tell me: why do you think she's in trouble?

PEARL: Well – she's been acting rather odd just recently.

ROBERT: What do you mean by "odd"? Do you mean she's been difficult; bad tempered?

PEARL: Good heavens, no! I've never known Eve lose her temper. I'm the bad-tempered one around here. No, it's just that – well, she's been terribly remote. Disinterested, I suppose you'd call it.

ROBERT: Disinterested in her work, you mean? In the shop?

PEARL: Yes. On Friday, for instance, she didn't come in at all. Nor on Saturday morning. I telephoned her flat and there was no reply. When she arrived on the Monday morning, I asked her what had happened and she just said she hadn't been feeling very well.

ROBERT: That's all she said?

PEARL: Yes. I tried to question her, but – she just wouldn't answer me.

ROBERT: I see. (*A moment*) Miss Mortimer … Pearl … I've known Eve a very long time and I'm sure I don't have to tell you that I'm extremely fond of her.

PEARL: We're both very fond of her.

ROBERT: (*Bluntly; almost curt*) Then tell me the truth. What is it you're worried about?

PEARL: I – I think in some curious sort of way she's mixed up with … what happened this morning.

ROBERT: The murder?

48

PEARL: Yes. Now please don't misunderstand me – for goodness' sake don't get me wrong! I don't, for one moment, think that Eve had anything to do with the murder; but, somehow, I don't think she was ...

ROBERT: Go on.

PEARL: I don't think she was completely surprised by it.

ROBERT: You mean – she knew that Lewis was going to be murdered?

PEARL: Yes – at least, that was my impression. You see, after I'd sent for the police, I telephoned Eve and told her what had happened. She was obviously shaken, very badly shaken, but she didn't seem terribly surprised by the news.

ROBERT: What did she say?

PEARL: It wasn't so much what she said, it ...

ROBERT: What <u>did</u> she say?

PEARL: She just said ... "Oh, my God." Nothing else. But it was the way she said it. So quietly; almost as if she wanted to say ... "Oh, my God – then it's happened, after all" ...

ROBERT: (*Thoughtfully*) I see.

PEARL: And there's something else too; something else I just don't understand. Whether it's got anything to do with the murder or not I wouldn't know, but ... Your sister, Katherine, bought a dress from us ... Oh, quite some time ago. Unfortunately, she lost the belt, and she wrote to Eve and asked her to try to get her another one exactly the same. We had difficulty, getting hold of the same material but eventually we succeeded and a little woman in Walton Street made the belt for us. I shall never forget the morning it arrived; Eve was so excited.

49

ROBERT: Why was she excited?

PEARL: I don't know. But believe me, she was – very excited. I just couldn't understand it.

ROBERT: (*Quietly*) You know what happened to the belt?

PEARL: Yes, she gave it to you to take to Venice, and for some reason or other, I can't imagine why, you gave it to your brother.

ROBERT: No, that's not true. She gave me the belt, yes – but I didn't give it to my brother.

PEARL: But they found it on him because the Inspector ...

ROBERT: Yes, I know. But I don't know what Lewis was doing with it.

PEARL: (*Puzzled*) But if you didn't give him the belt then who the devil ... (*Suddenly*) Here she is! Here's Eve!

Door opens; closes.

EVE: Robert!

ROBERT: Hello, Eve! (*Kisses her*)

EVE: I'm sorry I was out, Robert – I've just been to the chemist's.

ROBERT: I was late anyway; I didn't leave the Yard until after five, and then I dropped into the flat for a few minutes.

EVE: (*Tensely*) Robert, have they any idea – any idea at all – who did it?

ROBERT: No, I'm afraid they haven't – not yet.

PEARL: I can't imagine you telling us, if they had! Eve, Mrs Clayton phoned, she's in a flap about her coat. I'm taking it round straight away.

EVE: Yes, all right, Pearl. Here's the aspirin.

PEARL: Thank you, darling. Have you got some?

EVE: Yes, I bought two packets.

ROBERT: Eve, you look tired – and I'll bet you haven't had a bite to eat all day.

EVE: Pearl and I had a snack at lunch-time.

PEARL: You mean I had a snack at lunch-time! You didn't even drink your coffee. Take her out to dinner, Robert.

ROBERT: That's exactly what I intend to do.

EVE: I just couldn't eat a thing.

ROBERT: We'll see about that.

PEARL: I'll see you tomorrow, Eve. And don't bother to come in if you don't feel like it, just give me a ring.

EVE: Yes, all right, Pearl.

PEARL: And you can tell Sergeant Horton or Thornton or whatever his name is …

ROBERT: Thornton.

PEARL: … He can take my fingerprints here, tomorrow morning, at ten o'clock. And if he's five minutes late he'll be unlucky.

ROBERT: Thank you. I'll tell him.

Door opens; closes.

EVE: How are Katherine and Freddie?

ROBERT: They're both very well. Katherine's flying over tomorrow morning.

EVE: Was she terribly upset?

ROBERT: I think she was more stunned than anything else – we both were.

EVE: I know Katherine and Lewis never really got on well together, but – he was fond of her, Robert. He used to talk about her quite a lot when we were … in the old days.

ROBERT: Yes, I know. (*A moment*) Eve, what was Lewis doing here?

EVE: I – I don't know.

ROBERT: (*Quietly; quite simply*) Did you kill him?

51

EVE: (*Shocked*) Robert! Good God no! (*Near to tears*) Kill Lewis ...

ROBERT: Had you an appointment with him? Did you ask him to meet you here, at La Boutique?

EVE: No; I've told you, I don't know what he was doing here.

ROBERT: Are you sure, Eve?

EVE: Of course I'm sure! Do you think I'd lie to you?

ROBERT: You lied to a friend of mine.

EVE: What do you mean?

ROBERT: You told Inspector Daly that you didn't know Lewis was over here – that you didn't know he was in London.

EVE: Well ... I didn't.

ROBERT: Eve, my dear, that's not true. You know it's just not true. You told me, yourself, you'd seen a photograph of him in a newspaper. Besides, we talked about Lewis ... in the café ... just before I left for the airport.

EVE: Oh, yes – that's right. I – I forgot all about that. (*Suddenly: an attempt to change the subject*) Robert, have you got a cigarette? I'm afraid we're out of ...

ROBERT: (*Stopping her*) Eve, you've got to tell me what happened. You've got to tell me the truth.

EVE: (*After a moment; quietly distressed*) I've always been in love with Lewis...

ROBERT: Yes, I know that, Eve ...

EVE: I thought the divorce would make a difference. I thought once the divorce was over, and it was final I would feel differently towards him. I wanted to feel different, Robert. I wanted to hate him, really hate him for all the unhappiness he'd caused me. But I didn't ...

52

ROBERT:	(*Gently; yet firmly*) Eve, did you see Lewis?
EVE:	(*A momentary hesitation*) Yes.
ROBERT:	When?
EVE:	A couple of nights ago.
ROBERT:	Tell me about it. Tell me exactly what happened.
EVE:	He was on television, and I made it an excuse to phone him. He was pleasant, but a shade distant I thought, and when I put the phone down, I felt angry and just a little ashamed of myself for having ... contacted him again after all these years.
ROBERT:	Eve, for heaven's sake! Why shouldn't you have phoned Lewis if you wanted to?
EVE:	Anyway, that's how I felt. Then an hour later, very much to my surprise, he telephoned me. He said there'd been someone with him when I phoned, and he hoped I didn't think he'd been unfriendly. To cut a long story short he invited me out to dinner.
ROBERT:	And you went ...
EVE:	Yes.
ROBERT:	(*Exasperated*) Eve, for God's sake, why didn't you tell the Inspector about this?
EVE:	I don't know why. I lost my nerve ... He frightened me, Robert. I told one lie and then ... I got rattled.
ROBERT:	But don't you see, he'll find out about this dinner date. He's bound to, even if I don't tell him about it. Where did you have dinner?
EVE:	At the Savoy ...
ROBERT:	At the ... (*A worried sigh*) All right, Eve. Go on ...

EVE: I arrived at the hotel at about half past eight.
                (*Start Fade*) Lewis had a suite on the third floor
                facing the Embankment. As I walked down the
                corridor, I could hear a piano being played …

Complete Fade.

Fade in piano. Door opens. Piano stops.
PAGE BOY: (*Announcing*) Mrs Bristol, sir.
LEWIS: Eve!
EVE: Hello, Lewis …
Door closes.
LEWIS: Eve … Sweetie, how nice to see you! (*Kisses
                her*) And how very nice of you to come along
                like this. Let me take your coat … My – you
                look fabulous!
EVE: What was that tune you were playing?
LEWIS: Oh, it's something I wrote ages ago, for
                "Golden Girl"; but we never used it.
EVE: I thought I recognised it.
LEWIS: (*Sincerely; impressed*) Gee … You really do
                look wonderful, Eve. No kiddin' …
EVE: (*Pleased*) Thank you, Lewis.
LEWIS: What would you like to drink? A dry martini?
EVE: Please.
A pause.
LEWIS: (*Mixing drinks*) They tell me La Boutique's
                doing very well.
EVE: Who's "they"?
LEWIS: Robert.
EVE: Yes, it is.
LEWIS: I always said you were a very good business
                woman, Eve.
EVE: (*Thoughts elsewhere*) Yes, you did, didn't
                you, Lewis.

LEWIS: I hope this isn't going to be too dry for you.

EVE: (*Taking glass*) Thank you.

LEWIS: Well – here's to us, and a pleasant evening. Skoal! (*They drink*) I thought we'd dine in the restaurant; I've booked a table for half past nine so we've plenty of time. (*A pause*) Is the martini all right?

EVE: Yes, it's fine.

LEWIS: Not too dry?

EVE: No, it's perfect. (*Suddenly business-like*) What can I do for you, Lewis.

LEWIS: (*Completely taken aback*) What can you do for me?

EVE: Yes.

LEWIS: What do you mean?

EVE: (*Pleasantly*) Lewis, I knew the moment you phoned me, the moment I heard your voice, that you really wanted something from me. Do I really have to go through the whole evening wondering what it is?

LEWIS: My dear Eve, you really are the most extraordinary person! I haven't seen you for ages; I invite you out to dinner; I pay you a perfectly sincere and well-deserved compliment, and within five minutes you're accusing me of having a string of ulterior motives stretching from here to ... White Sulphur Springs! You really are incorrigible!

EVE: I'm never quite sure what incorrigible means, Lewis.

LEWIS: Well, in your case, Sweetie, it means an incurable habit of ...

EVE: ... Always being right about my ex-husband.

LEWIS: (*Laughing*) My God, I can't win, can I?

EVE: (*Quietly*) Lewis, I'm looking forward to this
           evening ...
LEWIS: So am I, my dear ...
EVE: Then whatever it is, tell me now. Let's get it out
           of the way before we go down to the restaurant.

A pause.

LEWIS: All right, Eve. You win. I'll tell you what I want
           you to do for me. But first, let's get one thing
           quite clear. This isn't why I asked you here, this
           isn't why I invited you to have dinner with me.
EVE: What is it you want, Lewis?
LEWIS: (*A moment*) You see this letter?
EVE: (*Puzzled*) Yes?
LEWIS: I want you to keep it for me until Thursday of next
           week. If you haven't heard from me by eleven
           o'clock on Thursday morning, post it. It's stamped
           and it's addressed.
EVE: But why don't you keep it, and post it yourself?
LEWIS: Oh, I'm frightfully careless these days, sweetie. I
           might lose it.
EVE: That's not very convincing, Lewis.
LEWIS: Will you do this for me?
EVE: Yes, of course I will. You simply want me to keep
           the letter ...
LEWIS: I want you to keep the letter until you hear from
           me. If you don't hear from me by eleven o'clock
           on Thursday morning, post it.
EVE: All right. Give it to me. I'll put it in my handbag.
LEWIS: Thank you, Eve.
EVE: But – is this all you want me to do?
LEWIS: Yes. Except that ... there's no need to mention
           this letter to anyone.
EVE: Why should I?

LEWIS: And if, by any chance, anything should happen to me – before Thursday, I mean … Well, just post the letter.

EVE: (*Surprised*) What do you mean – if anything should happen to you?

LEWIS: (*Obviously wishing to change the subject*) I might get knocked down by a bus or something. You know London, it's worse than New York these days. Eve, I'm going to have another dry martini. What about you?

EVE: (*Thoughtfully*) No, I haven't finished this one yet.

LEWIS: (*Slightly forced gaiety*) Well, come along, Eve! Drink up!

EVE: (*After a moment*) Lewis …

LEWIS: (*Mixing drink*) Yes, sweetie?

EVE: (*Changing her mind*) No. No, it doesn't matter …

LEWIS: What were you going to say?

EVE: It's not important. (*Quickly*) Lewis, would you like to do something for me now?

LEWIS: Yes, of course. What is it?

EVE: Play that number again; the one you were playing when I came in.

LEWIS: I'll do better than that, sweetie. I'll play you two new numbers, ones you've never heard before.

EVE: I'd rather hear the old … (*Resigned*) Yes, all right, Lewis …

A moment; the piano starts.
Fade piano.

EVE: (*Fade in*) … It was just gone ten o'clock when we went into the restaurant and the moment we reached our table the band started to play a selection from "Golden Girl". Lewis did his usual act of course – and everyone thought he was

57

embarrassed and irritated, but he was obviously loving every minute of it. I know I was. It was just like old times, Robert.

ROBERT: Go on, Eve.

EVE: I left the hotel at about a quarter to one, picked up a cab, and came straight here.

ROBERT: Why here – to the shop? Why didn't you go home?

EVE: We've got a safe here and I wanted to put the letter in it.

ROBERT: Did Lewis tell you to put it in the safe?

EVE: No, he didn't, but I was frightened of losing it.

ROBERT: I see. Did you ask him what was in the letter?

EVE: No, I only mentioned it once and that was while we were having coffee. I got the impression that he didn't really want to talk about it. So I didn't.

ROBERT: Who's it addressed to?

EVE: Someone in San Francisco. I think the name's Winter, but I'm not sure.

ROBERT: A Mr Rolf Winter?

EVE: (*Surprised*) Yes, that's right.

ROBERT: All right, Eve. Get me the letter.

EVE: (*Hesitating*) Robert, I don't want to be difficult, but I did promise Lewis that if anything should happen to him …

ROBERT: (*Gently; yet with authority*) Lewis is dead … I'll take care of the letter now, my dear.

EVE: Very well, Robert. The safe's in the basement. I won't be a minute.

Sound of footsteps; Eve descending to basement.

Telephone rings.

EVE: (*Calling*) Will you answer that, Robert?

ROBERT: (*Calling to Eve*) Yes, of course …

EVE: If it's for me, take a message!

ROBERT: (*Lifting receiver*) Hello?

CARL: (*On the other end; a crisp, faintly precise voice*) La Boutique?

ROBERT: Yes.

CARL: Could I speak to Mrs Bristol, please?

ROBERT: I'm sorry, she's not here just at the moment. Can I take a message?

CARL: (*Hesitating*) Well – er …

ROBERT: Who is it speaking?

CARL: It's Carl – a friend of hers. Tell Eve I'm sorry but I shan't be able to make it tomorrow after all. I'm having trouble with Berry.

ROBERT: With Barry?

CARL: (*Laughing*) No – Berry.

ROBERT: All right, I'll see she gets the message.

CARL: Thank you. (*Pleasantly*) Who is that, by the way?

ROBERT: My name's Bristol – Robert Bristol.

CARL: (*Faintly surprised*) Oh … Oh, yes, of course. Perhaps you'd be kind enough to give Eve my message?

ROBERT: Yes, I will.

CARL: Thank you, Mr Bristol. Goodbye …

ROBERT: Goodbye. (*Replaces receiver*)

A pause.

Sound of footsteps.

EVE: Who was that?

ROBERT: Someone called Carl. He says he's sorry but he can't make it tomorrow.

EVE: Oh …

ROBERT: He's having trouble with Berry – whatever that means.

EVE: They're both friends of mine. We were going to have lunch together …

ROBERT: I see.

59

EVE: (*Her thoughts elsewhere*) I'm afraid I'd forgotten all about it anyway …

ROBERT: (*Quietly*) May I have the letter, Eve?

EVE: What? (*Suddenly; almost as if she is pulling herself together*) Oh, yes, I'm sorry. Here it is. You were right about the name.

ROBERT: (*Taking the letter and looking at it*) Rolf Winter, c/o The Mark Hopkins Hotel, San Francisco …

EVE: Who's Rolf Winter?

ROBERT: He's an American; a millionaire.

EVE: Is he – was he a friend of Lewis's?

ROBERT: (*Studying the envelope*) No, not exactly a friend … Pass me those scissors, Eve.

EVE: Are you going to open the letter?

ROBERT: Yes, I am. (*Taking scissors*) Thank you. I'm opening it for two reasons. One; to satisfy my curiosity; and two: because there's no point in posting it to San Francisco anyway … (*Slits open letter*) Mr Winter's in London – at Claridge's.

EVE: In London? How do you know he's … (*Surprised*) It's a photograph.

ROBERT: (*Slowly*) Yes.

EVE: What is it? What's it a photograph of?

ROBERT: (*Quietly*) See for yourself, Eve.

EVE: Why … it's the shop! (*Bewildered*) Robert, why should Lewis send a photograph of my shop to someone I've never heard of? And why on earth…

ROBERT: Wait a minute! There's something else in the envelope – a note. (*Takes note from envelope*)

A pause.

EVE: What does it say? (*Puzzled*) Robert, what is it?

ROBERT: This is extraordinary! This note's written by Lewis, but it's supposed to have come from me.

60

EVE: From you?

ROBERT: Yes, it's signed "Robert Bristol". (*Reading*) "Dear Winter … Lewis has told me about the enclosed. If you want me to keep quiet about it do precisely as he tells you … Robert Bristol, Chief-Superintendent, C.I.D."

EVE: You're sure it's Lewis's handwriting?

ROBERT: Yes, there's no doubt about that. No doubt at all.

EVE: But why should Lewis put your name …

ROBERT: (*Interrupting her*) Eve, just a second, my dear. I want you to take a look at another photograph I've got. One very similar to this.

EVE: A photograph of La Boutique?

ROBERT: Yes. (*Takes out wallet*) Here it is …

EVE: (*A moment*) Where did you get this?

ROBERT: It was sent to me by someone – I don't know who – whilst I was in Venice. (*Quietly*) Now tell me: and be frank, Eve – have you seen either of these photographs before?

EVE: Well – yes … I have.

ROBERT: Who took them – do you know?

EVE: Pearl did; ages ago. It was after we'd seen some publicity in one of the newspapers about a new shop … that … was … opening … in Kensington.

ROBERT: (*Alarmed*) What is it, Eve? Are you all right?

EVE: I – I feel terribly faint. I think I'm going to … pass out …

ROBERT: Get hold of my arm!

EVE: Everything seems to be going round … and round … and …

ROBERT: Here we are – sit in this chair. Close your eyes, Eve … You'll feel better in a minute. Is there any brandy in the shop?

EVE: No, I don't think so, unless Pearl … It's all right … It's beginning to wear off … Don't worry, Robert. I feel better now. (*A pause*) I suddenly felt terribly dizzy … Everything started to go round and round …

ROBERT: It's not surprising. You've had a hell of a day and nothing to eat! Where's your coat?

EVE: It's over there. Why?

ROBERT: I'm taking you to a restaurant I know in Chelsea. It's a quiet little place and I'm sure …

EVE: Not tonight, Robert. I'd rather go home if you don't mind.

ROBERT: Eve, you've got to eat something, otherwise …

EVE: Take me home, Robert, please …

ROBERT: (*A moment; then:*) Yes, all right, my dear. Let me help you on with your coat.

Fade in Music.

Fade Music.
Door opens.

MRS WEBB: Excuse me, sir. Inspector Daly would like to see you. I told him you were still having breakfast   but he insisted on …

ROBERT: That's all right, Mrs Webb! (*Calling*) Come along in, Eric! (*To Mrs Webb*) Bring another cup, I expect the Inspector would like some coffee.

DALY: Sorry if I'm interrupting your breakfast …

ROBERT: No, I've just finished. Sit down, old boy.

MRS WEBB: Would you like a cup of coffee, sir?

DALY: No, not for me, thank you.

ROBERT: Are you sure, Eric?

DALY: Yes, quite sure, thank you.

ROBERT: (*Dismissing her*) That's all right, Mrs Webb. (*As door closes*) Well – is there any news?

DALY: Yes, there is, but – I'd like to have yours first.

ROBERT: Mine?

DALY: Yes. Didn't you see Mrs Bristol last night?

ROBERT: Yes, I saw her.

DALY: Well – what happened? Did she stick to her story about not having seen your brother?

ROBERT: No; she didn't. She saw Lewis all right; they even had dinner together.

DALY: (*Irritated*) Then why the devil didn't she tell me about it?

ROBERT: I don't know why. I think you must have rattled her.

DALY: I didn't rattle her; as a matter of fact she rattled me. She was so damned evasive.

ROBERT: (*Trying to change the subject*) Yes, well, anyway they had dinner together. Apparently, she saw him on television, rang him up, and he invited her round to his hotel.

DALY: I wish to God she'd told me this in the first place!

ROBERT: I agree. It was stupid of her not to. (*Suddenly*) Eric, I want you to do something for me. Find out all you can about a man called Rolf Winter. He's an American millionaire; he's probably staying at Claridge's at the moment. My brother met him in San Francisco and … Well, find out what you can about him. Now, what's your news?

DALY: You've heard of Hardy Nelson?

ROBERT: The pop singer? Who hasn't?

DALY: Well, he's appearing at the Savaranda club at the moment and …

ROBERT: The Savaranda? My brother used to play there.

DALY: When?

ROBERT: Oh, a long time ago. He was in the orchestra.

DALY: That was before he made his name as a composer?

ROBERT: Yes – it was before he started composing in fact. But what about Nelson?

DALY: Nelson usually arrives at the club about ten o'clock; but last night, for some reason or other, he didn't show up. At about half past twelve Anatole, the head waiter, strolled out into the alley at the back of the club. Apparently he usually pops out at about this time to get a breath of fresh air. Well, to cut a long story short, he saw a man's foot protruding from behind a dustbin. He investigated – and found Nelson. The poor devil was in a hell of a state. It was pretty obvious, even to Anatole, that he'd been very badly beaten up.

ROBERT: Go on, Eric.

DALY: Anatole was frightened; he sent for an ambulance, then telephoned his wife and told her to get in touch with me.

ROBERT: Why you?

DALY: Anatole and his wife have the flat below mine, we're quite friendly.

ROBERT: I see.

DALY: I arrived at the club just as they were taking Berry Nelson to the hospital. He was conscious but ...

ROBERT: (*Suddenly; surprised*) Berry?

DALY: Oh, I'm sorry. His professional name's Hardy, but everyone calls him Berry. He was conscious and obviously very scared, but he refused to make a statement. Then, just as the ambulance doors were closing, he said to Anatole ... "There's some money in my dressing room, Anatole – please take care of it for me" …

ROBERT: Go on.

DALY: We found two thousand three hundred pounds in his dressing room.

ROBERT: Good God!

DALY: We also found this …

ROBERT: But that's the belt that Eve gave me – the one you found on Lewis!

DALY: No; we've still got that at the Yard; this is another belt, Robert.

ROBERT: Another one? Has O'Hara seen this?

DALY: Not yet. We've got a meeting tonight. I tried to get hold of him first thing this morning, but he was in the Lab and wouldn't talk to me.

ROBERT: He's an impossible old devil! (*Looking at belt*) I must say, this belt looks the same as the other one to me, Eric.

DALY: Not when you get them side by side, it doesn't.

ROBERT: What's the difference? It's the same material.

DALY: Yes, but the buckle's slightly larger on this one.

ROBERT: It's thicker …

DALY: Yes. You see the name tab?

ROBERT: I'm just looking at it. (*Thoughtfully reading name*) La Boutique.

Telephone rings.

Pause.

Telephone continues ringing.

DALY: (*Quietly*) The phone, Robert.

ROBERT: (*His thoughts still somewhere*) What? Oh … Thank you … (*Lifts receiver*) Hello?

EVE: (*On the other end; tense, almost frightened at having made the call*) Robert?

ROBERT: (*Suddenly recognising her voice*) Is that you, Eve?

65

EVE:	Robert, I've got to see you! It's important! Could you come along to my flat straight away?
ROBERT:	Why, yes, of course. What is it, Eve? What's the matter?
EVE:	(*Near to tears*) I'll – I'll tell you when I see you, please come straight away, Robert …
ROBERT:	Yes, of course. Don't worry, Eve. I'll be with you in fifteen minutes. (*Replaces receiver.*)
DALY:	Mrs Bristol?
ROBERT:	Yes, and she's in a devil of a state by the sound of things.

Fade in Music.
Fade Music.

Fade in: elevator ascending.

DALY:	This seems a very pleasant block of flats.
ROBERT:	Yes, I think it's one of the nicest in St John's Wood. Eve only moved in here about a month ago.
DALY:	Which floor is Mrs Bristol on?
ROBERT:	The fourth.

Elevator stops.

DALY:	Is this the porter?
ROBERT:	Yes …

Elevator gates are opened and closed.

MORGAN:	Good morning, Mr Bristol.
ROBERT:	Hello, Morgan. How are you?
MORGAN:	I'm very well, thank you, sir. Mrs Bristol's out, sir. She went out about ten minutes ago.
ROBERT:	Are you sure?
MORGAN:	Yes, sir.
ROBERT:	But she's expecting us.

MORGAN:	Yes, I know, sir. She told me to tell you she'd had to rush down to the shop, sir – to La Boutique – she'd like you to join her there if possible.
ROBERT:	Oh, I see. Thank you, Morgan.
MORGAN:	Thank you, sir.
DALY:	(*To Robert*) I thought you said she sounded worried on the phone.
ROBERT:	She did. Very worried.
DALY:	Then I can't understand why she didn't wait until you…
ROBERT:	(*Interrupting him*) Just a minute, Eric! Morgan, did you see Mrs Bristol go out?
MORGAN:	No, sir – but I know she's gone.
ROBERT:	How do you know?
MORGAN:	Because she phoned me, sir, and said she was just leaving. That was ten minutes ago.
ROBERT:	But you didn't actually see her leave?
MORGAN:	How could I; I was in the basement? (*Faintly amused*) Mrs Bristol's out, sir. I told you – she's gone to the shop. I heard the car drive away.
ROBERT:	(*Apparently convinced*) Yes, all right. Thank you. Goodbye.
MORGAN:	Goodbye, sir.
A moment.	
DALY:	What is it, Robert?
MORGAN:	(*Puzzled*) Is anything the matter, Mr Bristol?
ROBERT:	(*Hesitant*) No, I don't think so, but … (*A sudden decision*) Come along, Eric – we're going up to the flat!

Sound of elevator gate opening and closing.
Fade.

Fade in front door bell ringing inside apartment.
Radio music in distant background.

DALY: She's out, I'm afraid …

ROBERT: Yes, it looks like it …

MORGAN: (*Faintly annoyed*) I told you, Mr Bristol – I
              heard the car drive away.

DALY: Wait a minute. (*Listening*) Is that the radio
              playing?

ROBERT: (*A moment; listening*) Yes …

MORGAN: She frequently leaves it on, sir. I heard it the
              other afternoon when she was out.

DALY: (*Puzzled*) What is it, Robert? What's
              worrying you?

ROBERT: I don't know, Eric. I don't know what the hell
              it is, but – there's something wrong. I feel
              there's something wrong somewhere. (*To
              Morgan*) Have you a key to this flat?

MORGAN: Yes, I've got a key to all the flats.

ROBERT: (*Quietly*) Open the door.

MORGAN: I – I don't know whether Mrs Bristol would
              like us to …

ROBERT: (*With authority*) Open it, Morgan.

MORGAN: Yes, sir.

*Door unlocked; as the door opens the telephone starts ringing
in the main room.*

DALY: There's the phone.

Fade up telephone ringing.

DALY: (*Entering room*) She's out, Robert. There's no
              one here.

ROBERT: Turn the radio off, Morgan.

Radio off; music stops. Telephone continues ringing.

DALY: (*Thoughtfully*) Robert …

ROBERT: Yes?

DALY:	Am I imagining things or … do you hear the sound of water?
ROBERT:	(*Listening*) Water? No … No, I don't think so …

Telephone still ringing.

MORGAN:	Shall I answer that, sir?
ROBERT:	Yes, go ahead, Morgan. No – wait a minute! I'll take it … (*Lifts receiver*) Hello? This is Robert Bristol …
VIRGINIA:	(*On the other end*) Mr Bristol?
ROBERT:	Yes … Who is that?
VIRGINIA:	(*A tense, urgent whisper*) Listen … Your sister-in-law's in the bathroom … They've given her an injection and put her in the bath …
ROBERT:	In the bath?
VIRGINIA:	Yes … For God's sale be quick, Mr Bristol! Be quick – or she'll drown. (*Rings off*)
DALY:	(*Alarmed*) Robert, what is it?
ROBERT:	Where's the bathroom? (*Desperately; shouting*) Morgan, where the hell's the bathroom?!

Fade Music in.
Music Fade.

End of Part Two

Part Three

MORGAN:	Shall I answer that, sir?
ROBERT:	Yes, go ahead, Morgan. No – wait a minute! I'll take it ... (*Lifts receiver*) Hello? This is Robert Bristol ...
VIRGINIA:	(*On the other end*) Mr Bristol?
ROBERT:	Yes ... Who is that?
VIRGINIA:	(*A tense, urgent whisper*) Listen ... Your sister-in-law's in the bathroom ... They've given her an injection and put her in the bath ...
ROBERT:	In the bath?
VIRGINIA:	Yes ... For God's sale be quick, Mr Bristol! Be quick – or she'll drown. (*Rings off*)
DALY:	(*Alarmed*) Robert, what is it?
ROBERT:	Where's the bathroom? (*Desperately; shouting*) Morgan, where the hell's the bathroom?!
MORGAN:	(*Puzzled*) It's through the hall, on the other side of the flat.
ROBERT:	(*Fade*) Come on, Eric ...

Fade in: Robert trying to open locked bathroom door.
Background noise of water.

ROBERT:	Eve! Eve, it's Robert! Eve, are you all right? ... The door's locked! We'll have to break it open ...
DALY:	Robert, what is it? What's happened?
ROBERT:	Morgan, is there a doctor here – in the block?
MORGAN:	Yes, there's a Dr Underdown on the fourth floor but I don't know whether he's in ...
ROBERT:	(*Trying to force the door*) Find him and bring him back here straight away – tell him it's urgent.
MORGAN:	(*Bewildered*) Yes, all right, Mr Bristol.

Robert throws his weight against the door.

DALY: You'll never break the door open that way! Wait a minute … Stand back and I'll kick the lock …

Daly kicks the door.

ROBERT: Try it again!

Daly kicks out again.

ROBERT: Here, let me try …

Robert kicks the door and lock snaps.

DALY: That's it.

ROBERT: Now give me a hand, Eric! (*Straining; forcing the door*) Come on … That's it… Steady …

The door breaks open. Noises of water pouring into bath.

DALY: What's the matter with her? Has she passed out?

ROBERT: Turn the water off!

Taps turned; water stops.

DALY: Robert, what the hell's happened?

ROBERT: Pass me that bathrobe … Quickly! … Get hold of her arms … That's it … now let's get her out of here and into the bedroom … Steady, Eric … (*Struggling; trying to lift Eve out of the bath*) Someone gave her an injection, put her in the bath, and then turned the water on …

DALY: Good God …

ROBERT: Put that other towel round her shoulders … Now get hold of her arms … That's right …

DALY: It's okay, I've got her …

ROBERT: Be careful … Steady, Eric, don't hit her shoulder on the door … That's it … Can you manage?

DALY: (*Start Fade*) Yes … I'm all right.

ROBERT: For God's sake don't slip …

74

Complete Fade.

EVE: (*Fade in*) … My head … Oh, my head … What … What happened? (*Confused and distressed*) Robert … have they gone? Have they left? (*Frightened*) Those two men ... are they … still here?

ROBERT: No – no, they've gone … It's all right, Eve.

DOCTOR: There's nothing to worry about, Mrs Bristol, just try and relax.

DALY: (*Quietly*) She's looking better, Robert.

ROBERT: Yes, thank goodness. (*Aside*) I thought she wasn't going to come round, Doctor.

DOCTOR: The drug's just beginning to wear off; she'll feel very much better in an hour or so. I have an appointment at ten o'clock. Can someone stay with her? I'd rather she wasn't left on her own, for the next hour or so at any rate.

MORGAN: She has a daily woman – a Mrs Kershaw – she should be here any minute now.

DOCTOR: Oh, good. I know Mrs Kershaw. She's very reliable.

ROBERT: I can stay until twelve, then I've got to go to the airport, I'm afraid. I'm meeting my sister.

DOCTOR: Just so long as she isn't left on her own … Now where the devil did I put that stethoscope? Oh, here we are …

DALY: Doctor, I think she's trying to say something …

DOCTOR: What is it, my dear?

EVE: (*With an effort; still distressed*) They – they had a key … They walked in … both of them … I thought they were just going to talk to me … I never realised they … (*In tears*)

75

DOCTOR: Now, please don't upset yourself, Mrs Bristol. You can tell us all about it later. It's not important. Right now I want you to try and forget what happened.

EVE: Yes, all right, Doctor.

DOCTOR: Come along, Superintendent. I think we'd better leave her.

MORGAN: I'll be in the lobby if you want me, sir.

ROBERT: Thank you, Morgan – and get the front door lock changed. That's important.

MORGAN: I'll see what I can do, sir.

DOCTOR: (*Start Fade*) Oh, just a second, Morgan. I'll give you a prescription and you can slip round to the chemist's with it. (*To Robert*) They're tablets, Mr Bristol. I want her to take two every four hours.

Complete Fade.

ROBERT: (*Fade in*) … Now come on, Eve … You can easily swallow these …

EVE: They look enormous.

ROBERT: No, they're not. Come on; here's a glass of water. Drink up.

Eve drinks; swallows tablets.

EVE: Thank you.

ROBERT: I'll take the glass.

EVE: I – I feel better than I did.

ROBERT: You look better.

EVE: Robert, how did you know I was in the bathroom? How did you know that …

ROBERT: (*Interrupting her*) Someone telephoned – I don't know who it was – and told me what had happened. Eve, do you feel like talking now, or would you rather wait until later?

EVE: There's not a lot to tell, Robert. It all happened so quickly. One moment I was standing by the telephone and the next ...

ROBERT: Start at the beginning, Eve.

EVE: I get a newspaper every day and this morning when I picked it up off the mat I saw a picture of a friend of mine – Berry Nelson – on the front page. Apparently he was attacked last night, beaten up, and the head waiter of the club ...

ROBERT: Yes, I know about Nelson. Go on, Eve. Tell me your story.

EVE: Well, someone has scribbled a message across the newspaper ... across Berry's photograph. Look, here we are, here's the paper ... (*Picks up newspaper; unfolds it*) Read it for yourself.

A pause.

ROBERT: (*Reading*) "This could happen to you – be careful" ... (*A moment*) Have you any idea who wrote this?

EVE: No.

ROBERT: You don't recognise the handwriting?

EVE: No; it looks like a woman's handwriting to me ...

ROBERT: ... Yes, I agree.

EVE: I didn't take the warning seriously at first. Then when I read the details, about Berry I mean ... when I realised exactly what had happened, how viciously he'd been beaten up. I became frightened and telephoned you.

ROBERT: Go on, Eve.

EVE: Just as I put the phone down, I heard the front door close. When I turned round, I saw two men standing in the hall. They said they wanted the letter, the one that Lewis gave me ... I told them I hadn't got it. (*Tensely*) I told them I'd given it to

you, but … they wouldn't believe me. Finally …
they made me phone Morgan …

ROBERT: To say you were just going out. Yes, I know.
Morgan told me. Go on, Eve.

EVE: (*Trying to control herself*) They questioned me for
ten minutes, Robert.

ROBERT: About the letter?

EVE: Yes, always about the letter. I thought they'd
never stop. I told them I'd given it to you; I swore
I'd given it to you … Then one of the men took a
syringe out of his pocket. He held it up so I could
see it … So I could see the needle.

ROBERT: The bastard …

EVE: I – I passed out.

ROBERT: Would you recognise either of these men, if you
saw them again?

EVE: I don't know. I might I suppose … I was so
frightened I … (*Suddenly*) Yes, I think I'd
recognise them.

ROBERT: (*Quietly*) Good.

Door opens.

MRS KERSHAW: May I come in?

ROBERT: Yes, come in, Mrs Kershaw.

MRS KERSHAW: I've just made a nice cup of tea, I thought
you might feel like one, dearie.

ROBERT: That's a very good idea, and you see she drinks it,
Mrs Kershaw. (*Start Fade*) I'll be back in a
moment, Eve. I'm just going into the lounge to
make a phone call.

Complete Fade.

*Fade in: Robert dialling a number: We hear the number
ringing out.*

GIRL: (*On the other end*) Claridge's Hotel …

ROBERT: Could I speak to Mr Rolf Winter, please? This is Superintendent Bristol.

GIRL: One moment. I'm not sure whether Mr Winter's available or not. (*A long pause*) I'm putting you through, sir.

ROBERT: Thank you.

WINTER: (*On the other end*) Hello?

ROBERT: Mr Winter?

WINTER: Speaking …

ROBERT: My name's Bristol, Mr Winter. Robert Bristol. I think you met my brother, Lewis, in San Francisco.

WINTER: Why, yes! I did. I sure did, Mr Bristol. And I was distressed, very distressed, sir, to read about … what happened to your brother.

ROBERT: Yes, well – I'm investigating the case, Mr Winter, and I think perhaps you might be able to help me.

WINTER: (*Puzzled*) Help you? If I can, I will, but in what way can I help you, Mr Bristol?

ROBERT: Well, for one thing, you can tell me about the letter.

WINTER: Letter? What letter?

ROBERT: (*After a momentary hesitation*) The photograph …

WINTER: Forgive me, but I'm sorry – I just don't seem to know what you're talking about.

ROBERT: (*Pleasantly*) In that case, may I call round this afternoon and explain what I'm talking about, Mr Winter?

WINTER: (*Still apparently puzzled*) Why, sure, if you think it'll be any help. I'll be delighted to see you – any time after four o'clock, Mr Bristol.

ROBERT: Shall we say half past four?

WINTER: Yes – that's okay.

ROBERT: Thank you. See you then, Mr Winter. (*Rings off*)

Fade in Music.

Fade Music.
Door opens.

NURSE: If you'll just wait in here for a few minutes, Inspector.

DALY: Yes, of course – thank you, Nurse. How is Nelson this morning?

NURSE: He's quite a bit better than we expected. Dr Casey seems quite pleased with him, in fact; incidentally, the doctor would like a word with you before you leave, Inspector.

DALY: Yes, of course.

NURSE: Mrs Nelson's with her husband at the moment, but she should be leaving any minute now.

DALY: Mrs Nelson?

NURSE: Yes.

DALY: I didn't realise he was married.

NURSE: Yes; they were married about two years ago. It was in all the papers. She's German; a very pretty girl.

DALY: But he lives on his own, he has a flat in Chelsea. I was there this morning.

NURSE: Yes, I know. They're separated. It was in the papers.

DALY: Obviously, the sooner I start reading the papers the better!

Door opens.

ELKA: (*A slight accent*) Excuse me. I think I left my coat in here.

NURSE: Yes, it's over here, Mrs Nelson.

ELKA: Thank you.

DALY: (*Picking up coat*) Allow me …

ELKA: (*Surprised*) Oh, thank you.

NURSE: I'll tell the doctor you're here, Inspector.

DALY: Thank you, Nurse.

Door closes.

DALY: Mrs Nelson, I'm Chief-Inspector Daly. Would you mind if I asked you a few questions about your husband?

ELKA: I'm – I'm sorry, but I have to be back at work by twelve o'clock.

DALY: It won't take a few minutes, Mrs Nelson.

ELKA: (*A moment*) What is it you want to know?

DALY: (*Pleasantly*) Well, obviously – I'd like to know who was responsible for what happened last night.

ELKA: I can't help you, I'm afraid. I don't know who was responsible. I – I just can't imagine why anyone should do a terrible thing like that.

DALY: I understand you're separated from your husband, Mrs Nelson?

ELKA: Yes, but – that's got nothing to do with this. Nothing at all. Berry and I – just decided to – What is the expression? ... Call it a day ...

DALY: You didn't have a row – a quarrel – over someone else?

ELKA: No, we didn't. There's no-one else. Certainly not so far as I'm concerned. I'm still very fond of my husband.

DALY: Then why did you separate?

ELKA: Do I have to discuss my personal affairs with you, Inspector?

DALY: (*Still friendly*) Mrs Nelson, at this precise moment, you don't have to discuss anything with me if you don't want to.

ELKA: (*After a moment*) Berry ... made a great deal of money very quickly. One of his recordings was in the top ten for several weeks. When you

81

DALY: suddenly make a lot of money, Inspector, you find you have a lot of friends. Brand new friends.

DALY: And you prefer old friends, is that it, Mrs Nelson?

ELKA: Yes. (*Thoughtfully*) Yes, that's just about it, I'm afraid. (*Suddenly*) Now, if you'll excuse me.

DALY: Yes, of course. If ever you want to get in touch with me, Mrs Nelson, you'll always find me at the Yard.

ELKA: (*Start Fade*) Why should I want to get in touch with you, Inspector? I've told you, I know nothing about ... what happened last night.

Complete Fade.

DALY: (*Fade in*) ... All right, Berry, I'll accept the explanation about the money. Although it sounds phoney to me.

BERRY: (*A Liverpool accent; early twenties*) What doesn't sound phoney to you, Inspector? You just don't believe a word I say.

DALY: When you start telling me the truth, I'll believe you.

BERRY: I've told you the truth! I won the money – gambling. Ask my manager, he was with me when I did it.

DALY: Then let's forget the money and talk about the belt.

BERRY: (*On edge*) I know nothing about the belt; I've never seen it before. I haven't a clue what it was doing in my dressing room.

DALY: (*Rising; abruptly*) Right. Thank you, Berry. I hope you'll feel better tomorrow.

BERRY: Wait a minute! Hold it! What's this all about, anyway? I was beaten up by a couple o' yobs who

	pinched my wallet and all you do is ask questions about a belt belonging to some bird or other.
DALY:	(*Quietly*) The belt was in your dressing room.
BERRY:	I know it was in my dressing room! You've told me that! But what's so important about a flaming belt? You know these night-clubs. There's always a lot of chicks hanging around. I expect one of 'em used my dressing room and left the belt there.
DALY:	I've questioned the girls. I've questioned everyone at the club. No-one's seen the belt before.
BERRY:	And neither have I.
DALY:	Right. Thank you, Berry.
BERRY:	Wait a minute! I still want to know what this is all about!
DALY:	(*A moment; then*:) A man called Lewis Bristol was murdered. His body was found in a dress shop. La Boutique. The shop belongs to his ex-wife.
BERRY:	Well?
DALY:	A belt – one like this – was found in his overcoat pocket.
BERRY:	(*Quietly; amazed*) In his pocket?
DALY:	Yes. Now you'll appreciate why I'm curious about this particular belt – the one found in your dressing room.
BERRY:	Yes. Yes, of course, but … (*Hesitates, then*:) Look, Inspector, I think there's something you ought to know. You'll find it out sooner or later anyway.
DALY:	Go on, Berry.
BERRY:	It just so happens that … Well, to be frank, I know Mrs Bristol – the woman who owns the dress shop.

DALY: She's a friend of yours?

BERRY: (*Quickly*) No, no, no, she's not a friend of mine,
          she's just an acquaintance.

DALY: How long have you known her?

BERRY: About six months, that's all. Carl – Carl May, my
          manager – is a friend of hers. She told him she
          was a fan of mine and he introduced us.

DALY: Did you ever meet Lewis Bristol, her ex-husband?

BERRY: No, never. Never set eyes on him. I gather he was
          a wolf and a half.

DALY: Who told you that?

BERRY: Carl. He hated Lewis Bristol. Hated his guts.
          (*Suddenly*) Oh – perhaps I shouldn't have said
          that.

DALY: When did you last see Mrs Bristol?

BERRY: A couple of weeks ago. Carl brought her to the
          club. Funny enough, we were all going to have
          lunch together today, but Carl couldn't make it.
          Still, I couldn't have made it either if it comes to
          that.

DALY: (*Quietly; about to depart*) Nor Mrs Bristol.

BERRY: What d'you mean?

DALY: She's ... indisposed at the moment. (*Turning
          away*) Well, I must be off! Take care of yourself,
          young man. Watch your figure. Don't over-eat.
          Remember your fans ...

BERRY: (*Laughing*) Oh, get lost, Inspector!

Fade in Music.

Fade Music.

*Fade in: background noises of Arrival Hall (European) at
London Airport.*

Announcement of Aircraft arrivals and departures.

ROBERT: (*Calling*) Katherine! Katherine, I'm over here!

KATHERINE: Hello, Robert!

ROBERT: My goodness, I thought I'd missed you. I had trouble parking the car. (*Kissing her*) I've only just arrived. Let me take your case.

KATHERINE: The plane was half an hour late, there was a delay in Venice.

ROBERT: How are you?

KATHERINE: Oh – I'm all right, considering.

ROBERT: I thought perhaps Freddie might have come with you.

KATHERINE: He was going to and then, at the last minute, I stopped him. I thought – well, what's the use? He didn't really know Lewis very well and he's terribly busy at the moment, and – anyway, I'd rather be on my own at a time like this.

ROBERT: Yes, I know. (*Gently*) I know, my dear.

KATHERINE: Is there any more news? How's Eve? How's she taken it? Have you discovered what Lewis was doing at …

ROBERT: (*Interrupting her*) I'll tell you all the news in the car. (*Start Fade*) Come along, Katherine.

Complete Fade.

Fade In: sound of car. Robert driving.

KATHERINE: …But this is incredible, Robert. Quite incredible! I can hardly believe it. Why should anyone want to … kill Eve?

ROBERT: They were after the letter. The one that Lewis gave her.

KATHERINE: Yes, but – I just don't understand it. And what's all this about the belt off my dress? If it is the same belt – then what was Lewis

85

doing with it? And how did he get hold of it in the first place?

ROBERT: I don't know. Eve gave it to me. I packed it – I was sure I packed it – and then it disappeared. The next thing I knew, Lewis had it. (*Suddenly*) Katherine, tell me about this belt – about the dress. When did you buy it?

KATHERINE: Oh, about eighteen months ago. I usually buy something from La Boutique when I'm over here. Eve showed me this particular dress and … No, no, that's not true. Now I come to think of it she was out when I called at the shop and her assistant – a girl called Simone – showed it to me.

ROBERT: Simone?

KATHERINE: Yes, a Belgian girl. She used to work at La Boutique.

ROBERT: That's right! I remember her now. A good-looking girl.

KATHERINE: I believe she left about six months ago. Anyway, I was crazy about the dress, and I bought it.

ROBERT: And a little while later you lost the belt?

KATHERINE: I think I must have lost it almost immediately, but I didn't discover the fact until quite some time later.

ROBERT: Why was that?

KATHERINE: It was a summer dress and the weather changed almost as soon as I bought it.

ROBERT: You mean, you didn't wear the dress straight away?

KATHERINE: No, I packed it and then when I got home, I put it in the wardrobe. Several weeks later,

	when I wanted to wear it, I noticed the belt was missing.
ROBERT:	(*Thoughtfully*) I see.
KATHERINE:	Robert, I'm worried about Eve. Do you think she'll be all right?
ROBERT:	Yes. Yes, I'm sure she will.
KATHERINE:	Could we drive round there straight away?
ROBERT:	Yes, of course, if you want to. Suppose I drop you there and you meet me at my place later?
KATHERINE:	Yes, that's all right. That suits me fine.
ROBERT:	It would suit me, Katherine, because I want to see Pearl Mortimer some time today and I've several appointments this afternoon. (*Start Fade*) I'll probably be back at my flat by about half past five …

Complete Fade.

PEARL:	(*Fade in*) … Robert, I know you think I'm being difficult and that I don't want to answer your questions, but Inspector Daly was here this morning and he asked me precisely the same questions you're asking!
ROBERT:	Yes, I imagine he did.
PEARL:	(*Not bad-tempered*) Then for heaven's sake talk to the Inspector and not me!
ROBERT:	I'm sorry, Miss Mortimer, but …
PEARL:	Pearl, please …
ROBERT:	I'm sorry, Pearl, but it's you I want to talk to, not the Inspector.
PEARL:	Look – I want to help you, Robert. I'd really like to help you, but I just don't know anything about this business.
ROBERT:	By "this business" you mean the murder, and what happened to Eve?

PEARL: Yes, of course.

ROBERT: Then … you think there's a connection?

PEARL: What do you mean? Good heavens, of course there's a connection! (*Telephone rings*) Even if Eve hadn't told me about the letter, the photograph, I'd have been convinced that …

Telephone ringing.

ROBERT: When did Eve tell you about the photograph?

PEARL: Excuse me. (*Lifts receiver*) La Boutique … I beg your pardon? (*Curtly*) I'm sorry, you've got the wrong number. (*Replaces receiver*)

ROBERT: (*Quietly*) When did Eve tell you about the photograph?

PEARL: This morning. As soon as the Inspector left. I closed the shop and rushed round to see her. Naturally, I was worried about her. Terribly worried.

ROBERT: Did she … tell you anything else?

PEARL: Why, yes! She told me about the two men, the girl on the phone, the letter with your name on it addressed to Rolf Winter. She told me everything, in fact.

ROBERT: Had you heard of Mr Winter before?

PEARL: Yes; at least, I think so. I seem to remember Carl May mentioned him a long time ago.

ROBERT: In what connection?

PEARL: I don't know. I can't remember …

ROBERT: Carl May. He's a friend of Eve's?

PEARL: Yes; he and Berry Nelson are great friends of hers. I can't imagine why. It's always been a mystery to me. Quite apart from thinking he's God's gift to womanhood, May's a snob, and a pretty bitchy one into the bargain. And Berry, well – he's just a glorified wide-boy. Although I must say, I feel pretty sorry for the poor devil at the moment, being beaten up like that.

ROBERT: (*Thoughtfully*) Carl May telephoned Eve the other night, when I was here …

PEARL: That doesn't surprise me; he frequently phones her.

ROBERT: What is he? What does he do exactly?

PEARL: He owns the Savaranda Club and he manages three or four pop groups – and Hardy Nelson, of course.

ROBERT: Nelson must be a money-spinner.

PEARL: You can say that again! I wouldn't mind ten per cent of him. Come to think of it, that's just about as much as I could take of the little horror.

ROBERT: Is May a wealthy man?

PEARL: It's difficult to tell. He's just bought a house in Eaton Square. I suppose he must be wealthy.

ROBERT: M'm. (*Suddenly*) Pearl, tell me: when Eve mentioned the photograph did she say what it was a photograph of?

PEARL: Why, yes, of course. And frankly, at first, I just didn't believe her. It sounded absurd. A photograph of La Boutique! I ask you, why on earth should anyone attach importance to a photograph of a dress shop? Have you got the photograph on you, by the way?

ROBERT: Yes, I have. (*Takes photograph out of pocket*) Here it is … (*A long pause*) Eve told me you took it …

PEARL: Yes, I did.

ROBERT: Did you take this one as well?

A pause.

PEARL: Yes. (*Puzzled*) Where did you get that?

89

ROBERT: (*Ignoring her question*) How many photographs did you take?

PEARL: Of La Boutique? About ten or twelve. We picked the best two and then had prints made. We sent prints all over the place. Dozens of 'em.

ROBERT: Why?

PEARL: Why? (*Laughing*) Because we wanted publicity and we couldn't afford a P.R.O.

ROBERT: I see.

Door opens.

PEARL: But how your brother Lewis managed to get hold of one, I can't imagine. Unless, of course, Eve sent it to him.

CUSTOMER: Good afternoon, Miss Mortimer.

PEARL: Oh, good afternoon, Mrs Whiting. (*To Robert*) Will you excuse me?

ROBERT: Yes, of course. Thank you, Pearl. You've been very helpful.

PEARL: Have I? Then I must be slipping. I'm not the helpful type as a rule.

ROBERT: (*Smiling*) Goodbye …

PEARL: What can I do for you, Mrs Whiting?

CUSTOMER: (*Start Fade*) I told Mrs Bristol I'd call in this morning. I'm afraid the dress I bought from you last week needs a slight alteration.

Complete Fade.

Fade in typewriter. Door opens and closes.
Typewriter stops.

WINTER: Have you finished?

BETTY: Yes, Mr Winter. It's ready for signing. (*Takes letter out of machine*)

WINTER: What about the letters I dictated this afternoon?

BETTY: They'll go off first thing tomorrow morning.

90

WINTER: Good.

BETTY: Mr Bristol's on his way up, they've just telephoned.

WINTER: Leave us alone for ten minutes and then give him the usual brush-off.

BETTY: Right ... Here we are, sign this.

A knock; door opens.

WINTER: Come in! (*Turning; suddenly affable*) Mr Bristol?

ROBERT: Yes ...

WINTER: I'm Rolf Winter. (*Shaking hands*) Nice to make your acquaintance. All right, Betty, see you later. Oh, where's Mrs Winter?

BETTY: She's out shopping, sir ...

WINTER: (*Chuckling*) No, you don't say!

BETTY: ... She said she'd be back by five o'clock.

WINTER: Okay! Sit down, Mr Bristol. When my wife walks into a store, they think it's a take-over bid. Now, can I get you a drink? A dry martini?

ROBERT: No, thank you.

WINTER: Are you sure?

ROBERT: Yes, I'm quite sure, thank you.

WINTER: Well – do you mind if I have one?

ROBERT: No, of course not. Go right ahead.

WINTER: (*Mixing himself a drink*) I was very shocked when I read about your brother, Mr Bristol. Have the police any idea who did it?

ROBERT: No; but it's early days yet. That's why I wanted to see you, I think perhaps you may be able to help me.

WINTER: Well, if I can help you, I certainly will, but I can't imagine how. I hardly knew your brother; so far as I remember I only met him twice.

ROBERT: When was that?

WINTER: Oh – a few weeks ago.

ROBERT: In San Francisco?

WINTER: Yes.

ROBERT: Tell me about it.

WINTER: There's nothing much to tell. Skoal. (*Drinks*) A man called John G. Reynolds tried to interest me in a film proposition; he brought your brother along. To cut a long story short, I disliked the proposition and I disliked Reynolds even more. After they'd left, I realised I'd been pretty rude to your brother so I phoned him, apologised, and invited him to a party I was giving.

ROBERT: Did you get a chance to talk to Lewis at the party?

WINTER: Yes, of course. So far as I remember we talked about Hollywood; his show "Golden Girl"; about television … He was an interesting man, Mr Bristol. And charm? He sure had more than his share of charm.

ROBERT: Yes. I don't think anyone could dispute that. And that was the last time you saw my brother?

WINTER: It was the only time I saw him, apart from the interview with Reynolds. Now perhaps you'll tell me something. What were you talking about on the phone? Unless I misunderstood you, you said something about a photograph and a letter.

ROBERT: Yes. Shortly before he was murdered Lewis gave his ex-wife a letter. It was addressed to you at the Mark Hilton hotel in San Francisco.

WINTER: Addressed to me?

ROBERT: He told Eve, Mrs Bristol, that if anything should happen to him the letter had to be posted.

WINTER: Go on …

ROBERT: After the murder I took possession of the envelope and opened it. (*Takes out photograph*) This photograph was inside it.

WINTER: And nothing else?

ROBERT: Yes – there was this note. Read it …

WINTER: (*Reading to himself*) "Lewis had told me about the enclosed. If you want me to keep quiet about it do precisely as he …" But you wrote this!

ROBERT: No, it's Lewis's handwriting, he put my name to it.

WINTER: But why? Look, I'm sorry, I don't get this! What is this photograph – what is this place, anyway?

ROBERT: It's a shop.

WINTER: Yes, I can see that. I can see the name on it. La … Bou … tique …

ROBERT: It's a dress shop in Marsham Square just off Sloane Street.

WINTER: (*Suddenly, amused*) Why, for Pete's sake, should your brother want to send me a photograph of a dress shop?

ROBERT: (*Pleasantly*) I was hoping you'd be able to explain that, Mr Winter.

WINTER: I'm sorry. I just haven't the slightest idea what this is all about. You say he gave this letter to Mrs Bristol?

ROBERT: Yes.

WINTER: Well – why didn't he post it himself?

ROBERT: He was due to leave for San Francisco next Monday, so I imagine he wanted it posting after he'd left.

WINTER: Yes, but why?

ROBERT: That's a good question, Mr Winter. I wish I knew the answer. (*Rising*) Anyway, obviously you've never heard of La Boutique and can't help me. I know you're a busy man, sir – so I won't take up any more of your time.

93

WINTER:	No, no, wait a minute! I've an idea! Why don't you make inquiries at the dress shop; maybe they could help you? Perhaps the people who own it...
ROBERT:	Mrs Bristol owns it.
WINTER:	(*Surprised*) You mean – the woman your brother gave the letter to? His ex-wife?
ROBERT:	Yes.
WINTER:	Now let's get this straight. Let's make sure I understand this. (*Slowly*) Your brother gave his ex-wife a photograph of her own shop – La Boutique – and told her to post it to me?
ROBERT:	That's right. Except of course she didn't know about the photograph, or the note, until the envelope was opened.
WINTER:	Well, what happened when you opened the envelope?
ROBERT:	She was very surprised.
WINTER:	I can well believe it! (*Door opens*) I can <u>well</u> believe it, Mr Bristol.
VIRGINIA:	Oh, I'm sorry! I didn't know you had someone with you.
WINTER:	Come in, Virginia!
VIRGINIA:	No, no, it's all right, Rolf. I'll ...
WINTER:	Come in, Virginia! Come in! I'll take your parcels, honey. (*Taking parcels*) Have you been shopping all afternoon?
VIRGINIA:	No; I went to the cinema for a couple of hours.
WINTER:	Oh, I beg your pardon. This is my wife. Honey, this is Mr Bristol – Superintendent Bristol, I should say.
ROBERT:	Hello, Mrs Winter. I'm glad to meet you. I think you met my brother in San Francisco.

94

VIRGINIA:	(*Vaguely*) Your brother?
ROBERT:	Yes – Lewis …
VIRGINIA:	I'm sorry, I …
WINTER:	You remember, honey. It was in the papers about … Lewis Bristol. We were talking about him only the other night. (*To Robert*) I don't think my wife actually met Lewis, Mr Bristol. She was late turning up at the party that night and your brother had already left. I might add that was before we were married. She's more punctual these days, aren't you, honey?
VIRGINIA:	Yes. That's one thing I've learnt on my honeymoon, Mr Bristol, if nothing else. To be punctual.

An awkward pause.

WINTER:	Honey, Mr Bristol's been asking me about a dress shop in Marsham Mews called La Boutique. I was wondering if, by any chance … (*Stops*) I'm sorry, I mean Marsham Square.
ROBERT:	No, as a matter of fact you're right. The shop is in Marsham Mews. I made a mistake.
WINTER:	Oh … Well, I was just wondering if you'd heard of it, honey?
VIRGINIA:	La Boutique? There's hundreds of dress shops called La Boutique.
ROBERT:	Yes, I know. This one belongs to my sister-in-law, Eve Bristol.
VIRGINIA:	(*A moment*) No, I've never heard of it. (*Ignoring Robert*) Rolf, will you excuse me? I'm very tired and if we're going to the theatre tonight, I'd really like a rest beforehand.

WINTER: Yes, of course, baby. Our friend's just leaving anyway.

VIRGINIA: (*Still vague; off-hand*) Good-bye, Mr Bristol. Nice to have met you.

ROBERT: (*Looking at her*) Goodbye, Mrs Winter. Nice to have met you too.

Fade in Music.

Fade Music.

Fade in: Robert unlocking his front door.

Door suddenly opens from inside.

KATHERINE: Oh, it's you, Robert!

ROBERT: Hello, Katherine!

KATHERINE: My, you look wet!

ROBERT: It's pouring outside. Where's Mrs Webb?

KATHERINE: She's in her room changing. I gave her the afternoon off and she's just got back. I hope you didn't mind?

ROBERT: (*Taking his things off*) I know, she talked your head off and you couldn't take it!

KATHERINE: (*Laughing*) You're not far wrong. It's all right, I'll hang those up.

ROBERT: Come along, let's go into the lounge.

Fade.

Fade in:

ROBERT: … What time did you get back from Eve's?

KATHERINE: Oh, about half past two.

ROBERT: How was she?

KATHERINE: Better than I expected. The doctor called when I was there. He seemed quite pleased with her.

ROBERT: Oh, good.

KATHERINE: I said we'd drop in this evening.

ROBERT: Yes, of course.

KATHERINE: Robert, I've got something to tell you. A rather curious thing happened this afternoon.

ROBERT: Curious? In what way, curious?

KATHERINE: Well – when I got back from Eve's I felt tired and pretty miserable so I told Mrs Webb I was going to bed for an hour or two and she could have the afternoon off.

ROBERT: Go on, Katherine.

KATHERINE: I'd been in bed about ten minutes or so when the doorbell rang. (*Start Fade*) At first I thought … Oh, hell, let it ring … and then, I don't quite know why, I decided to answer it …

Complete Fade.

Fade in: doorbell ringing. Bell continues. Door opens.

VIRGINIA: (*Tense; distinctly nervous*) Excuse me … Could I speak to Mr Bristol, please …?

KATHERINE: I'm sorry, but he's out at the moment.

VIRGINIA: When are you expecting him back?

KATHERINE: I'm not sure. Later this afternoon, I think, or … early this evening. (*Puzzled*) Excuse me – haven't we met before somewhere?

VIRGINIA: I – I don't think so.

KATHERINE: Well – can I take a message? I'm Mrs Hauptmann, Robert's sister.

VIRGINIA: Oh, of course! You're Katherine!

KATHERINE: (*Still puzzled*) Yes, I'm Katherine …

VIRGINIA: You probably saw me in Venice, Mrs Hauptmann. At your hotel. We – my husband and I – had dinner there several times. I'm Virginia All … I beg your pardon, Winter.

KATHERINE: Oh, yes – of course. You were a friend of
Lewis …
VIRGINIA: (*A moment, then:*) That's right. May I come
in, Mrs Hauptmann, I'd like to talk to you?
Hall clock suddenly chimes; three o'clock.
KATHERINE: Yes … Yes, of course. Please do …
Door closes.
Fade on clock chiming.

VIRGINIA: (*Fade in*) … I felt dreadful about Lewis,
really dreadful. But I knew in my heart of
hearts that it would never have worked.
Believe me, it wasn't that I didn't like Lewis.
I was terribly fond of him, but …
KATHERINE: (*Interrupting her; obviously somewhat
confused*) Mrs Winter, forgive me – but is this
why you wanted to see my brother? Simply to
tell him why … you decided not to marry
Lewis?
VIRGINIA: No – no, I … think there's something your
brother ought to know.
KATHERINE: About what?
VIRGINIA: About Lewis and … (*Hesitates*)
KATHERINE: Go on, Mrs Winter.
VIRGINIA: One night Lewis and I were having a drink
together in a restaurant in Sausalito, that's just
across the bay from San Francisco. The
restaurant was crowded, and we were waiting
for a table for dinner. A dark, rather attractive
looking man came out of the dining room and
although I'd never seen him before I knew
immediately that he was no stranger to Lewis.
I asked your brother if he was a friend of his
and he said, quite vehemently, "A friend of
98

mine! That man! Good God, Virginia, we hate each other's guts!"

KATHERINE: Go on …

VIRGINIA: The man collected his coat and was almost out of the restaurant when he suddenly spotted Lewis and came across to our table. Even before he spoke Lewis was angry. His hand was shaking and for one horrible moment I thought he was going to throw his drink in the man's face.

KATHERINE: But who was this man? And what did he say?

VIRGINIA: He said, "Hello, Lewis. Written any good numbers lately?" Then he turned and just walked away.

KATHERINE: That's all he said?

VIRGINIA: That's all. But it certainly had an effect on Lewis. He was shaking with anger; he could barely speak in fact. After a little while I asked him who the man was and he said his name was Carl May and that he lived in London.

KATHERINE: Carl May?

VIRGINIA: Yes.

KATHERINE: I've never heard of him. Is that all Lewis told you about him – that he lived in London?

VIRGINIA: Yes. All through dinner I tried to find out why they hated each other so much, but Lewis wouldn't tell me. Then later in the evening, just as we were getting into his car, he said: "I'll tell you one thing, Virginia. If ever I'm found with a knife in my back, the first man to question will be Carl May" …

KATHERINE: (*Shocked*) He … said that?

VIRGINIA: Yes – and that's why I came here this afternoon. That's what I wanted to tell Superintendent Bristol.

KATHERINE: I see. (*Curious*) Does your husband know that you …

VIRGINIA: My husband doesn't know anything about this, Mrs Hauptmann – and, please, I'd rather he didn't. (*Suddenly*) Now, if you'll excuse me. I hope you'll tell your brother, Robert, what I've just told you.

KATHERINE: Yes, I shall, of course – but he'll want to see you. (*Start Fade*) He'll want to talk to you himself. Where are you staying in London?

VIRGINIA: We're at Claridge's, but I'd rather he didn't phone me …

Complete Fade.

KATHERINE: (*Fade in*) … Mrs Winter said she didn't want you to phone in case her husband took the call, but she'd try and ring you herself sometime tomorrow morning. Whether she will or not, I don't know.

ROBERT: I see. Thank you, Katherine.

KATHERINE: Robert, have you heard of this man – Carl May – before?

ROBERT: Yes, I have. He's a friend of Eve's, and he owns the Savaranda Club. Years ago Lewis used to work there. (*Suddenly*) Katherine, what was she like, this woman? Describe her to me.

KATHERINE: (*Surprised by the question*) Mrs Winter? She was tall … good looking … blonde … I suppose she's about twenty-seven or eight.

	She had a tense, strange sort of manner, I thought.
ROBERT:	And what was she wearing?
KATHERINE:	A pink suit with a pink and white blouse and she had a diamond brooch – in the shape of a leaf – on one of her lapels.
ROBERT:	Thank you. (*Satisfied*) It's the same woman.
KATHERINE:	(*Puzzled*) What do you mean?
ROBERT:	I wanted to make sure, quite sure, that it was Mrs Winter you saw. It's her all right. I saw her myself about an hour ago.
KATHERINE:	(*Surprised*) Where?
ROBERT:	At Claridge's; I went to see her husband.
KATHERINE:	Did she say anything? Did she say that she'd been trying to get in touch with you?

Door opens.

ROBERT:	No. She said very little. Her husband was there all the time and she pretended she hardly knew Lewis. Yes, what is it, Mrs Webb?
MRS WEBB:	Excuse me, sir – there's a gentleman to see you.
ROBERT:	Well – who is it, Mrs Webb?
MRS WEBB:	I don't know the gentleman, sir – but here's his card.
ROBERT:	(*Taking card*) Thank you.

A pause.

KATHERINE:	(*Curious*) Who is it, Robert?
ROBERT:	It's Carl May …

Fade in Music.

Fade Music.

End of Part Three

Part Four

MRS WEBB: Excuse me, sir – there's a gentleman to see you.

ROBERT: Well – who is it, Mrs Webb?

MRS WEBB: I don't know the gentleman, sir – but here's his card.

ROBERT: (*Taking card*) Thank you.

A pause.

KATHERINE: (*Curious*) Who is it, Robert?

ROBERT: It's Carl May ...

KATHERINE: Carl May!

ROBERT: Yes. (*A moment*) Ask the gentleman to come in, Mrs Webb.

MRS WEBB: Yes, sir.

Door closes.

KATHERINE: What do you think he wants, Robert? Why do you think he's come to see you?

ROBERT: I don't know. Unless he's heard about this morning, and he's worried about Eve.

KATHERINE: Is he a great friend of hers?

ROBERT: (*Slightly irritated by the question and the thought*) I told you: according to Miss Mortimer he is.

Door opens.

MRS WEBB: Mr May, sir.

CARL: Superintendent Bristol? I apologise for calling unexpectedly like this. It's very kind of you to see me.

ROBERT: This is my sister – Mrs Hauptmann.

KATHERINE: Good evening.

CARL: Mrs Hauptmann, forgive me for this intrusion but I won't keep your brother long.

KATHERINE: That's all right, Mr May. Excuse me, Robert. I want to have a word with Mrs Webb.

ROBERT: Yes, all right, Katherine.

Door opens and closes.

ROBERT: Sit down, Mr May. Would you care for a drink?

CARL: (*Hesitates; then:*) Thank you, no ... (*Sits down*) But I'd like a cigarette. May I help myself?

ROBERT: Please do.

CARL: Thank you. (*Takes cigarette; uses lighter*)

ROBERT: Now what can I do for you?

CARL: May I speak frankly, and come straight to the point?

ROBERT: I'd prefer that you did.

CARL: I knew your brother Lewis. Many years ago he used to work for me at the Savaranda Club. (*A moment, then:*) I disliked him, Mr Bristol. Disliked him intensely.

ROBERT: (*Politely*) Is that what you came here to tell me?

CARL: No; I came here to tell you that, in spite of my feelings towards Lewis – I didn't kill him.

ROBERT: Has anyone suggested that you did?

CARL: No, not exactly ...

ROBERT: What does that mean – not exactly?

CARL: A colleague of yours – Inspector Daly – questioned a friend of mine this morning.

ROBERT: ... Hardy Nelson?

CARL: Yes; Hardy Nelson. Unfortunately, Berry – his friends call him Berry – told the Inspector that I hated your brother and ... Well, I just don't want the Inspector, or anyone else, to jump to conclusions because of that, to say the least, extremely tactless remark.

ROBERT: We try very hard not to jump to conclusions, Mr May.

CARL: Just because you dislike a person it doesn't mean to say that you want to kill them.

ROBERT: It doesn't indeed. (*A pause; politely*) Is there anything else you'd like to tell me?

CARL: There's something I'd like to ask you, Mr Bristol.

ROBERT: Go ahead.

CARL: The Inspector questioned Berry because he was beaten up last night.

ROBERT: That's right.

CARL: Now, personally, I don't think the beating up was of any particular significance, apart from the fact that Berry lost his wallet, of course. That sort of thing goes on the whole time, especially in London. But from what I gather your friend the Inspector seems to be trying to tie up the Berry Nelson incident with the death of your brother.

ROBERT: There is a tie-up, Mr May.

CARL: You mean the belt, that was found in his dressing room?

ROBERT: Yes.

CARL: But Berry doesn't know anything about the belt.

ROBERT: Perhaps he doesn't, but there's still the tie-up, still the connection.

CARL: Surely, it's just a coincidence, that's all?

ROBERT: Just <u>another</u> coincidence?

CARL: What do you mean – just another one?

ROBERT: Mr May, let's take a look at the facts. Berry Nelson was very nearly murdered last night. In his dressing room was found a belt off a girl's dress. Berry says he's never seen the belt before and he can't account for it being in his dressing room. But exactly the same sort of belt was found in …

CARL: Your brother's overcoat pocket …

ROBERT: Exactly. And my brother's body was found at La Boutique, which is where the two belts originally came from.

CARL: Yes, I know.

ROBERT: Well, did you know that less than twelve hours after the attack on your friend Berry Nelson, someone also tried to murder your friend Eve Bristol?

CARL: (*Astonished*) No, I didn't! You mean – she was beaten up?

ROBERT: No; she wasn't beaten up. But someone certainly tried to kill her; she's lucky to be alive.

CARL: Good God! Poor Eve … Is she all right?

ROBERT: Yes, she is now, but the bastards gave her a pretty rough time of it.

CARL: But why should anyone want to kill Eve?

ROBERT: She had a letter, or rather an envelope, which was given to her by my brother. Two men went to her flat and tried to get it from her.

CARL: And did they get it?

ROBERT: No; fortunately, she'd already given it to me.

CARL: A letter from your brother?

ROBERT: Yes; addressed to a man called Rolf Winter.

CARL: I seem to have heard that name.

ROBERT: He's an American, from San Francisco.

CARL: That's probably where I heard it; I was over there a couple of weeks ago. Curiously enough, that was the last time I saw Lewis.

ROBERT: In San Francisco?

CARL: Yes; he was in a restaurant.

ROBERT: Did you speak to him?

CARL: (*After a moment*) Yes, I spoke to him.

ROBERT: Mr May, tell me: why did you and Lewis hate one another so much?

CARL:	I don't know why he hated me. I can only tell you why I hated him.
ROBERT:	Why?
CARL:	(*A momentary hesitation*) Because he was a phoney – and a cheat.
ROBERT:	What do you mean – a cheat?
CARL:	He used to buy songs from other people – from other composers – and pass them off as his own.
ROBERT:	I don't believe that!
CARL:	It's true. I despised him! I hated his guts! (*Looking at Robert*) But I didn't kill him, Mr Bristol.

Fade in Music.
Fade down Music.

Fade in: street noises.
Robert and Katherine are walking along the pavement.

KATHERINE:	(*Almost a shade angry*) … I don't believe it about Lewis! I refuse to believe it!
ROBERT:	(*Worried*) Well, I must say May sounded convincing.
KATHERINE:	I don't give a damn how convincing he sounded! Lewis wrote every single note of "Golden Girl", I'm sure of that.
ROBERT:	May didn't specifically mention "Golden Girl", Katherine. He simply said …
KATHERINE:	(*Indignantly*) Well, it was "Golden Girl" that made Lewis! If it hadn't have been for "Golden Girl" no-one would have heard of him.
ROBERT:	Yes, I know, but … (*Laughing, in spite of himself*) Katherine, I'm not disagreeing with you about this. I'm sure you're right, but …

KATHERINE: (*Interrupting*) But, what?

ROBERT: (*Taking her arm*) The car's on the other side of the road. Watch the kerb.

KATHERINE: But, what, Robert?

ROBERT: Do you remember what Mrs Winter told you? Do you remember what May said to Lewis when he saw him in the restaurant that night?

KATHERINE: No, what did he say?

ROBERT: "Hello, Lewis. Written any good numbers lately?"

KATHERINE: Well, that's doesn't mean anything. It's just the smart Alec remark that a man like May would make.

A pause.

ROBERT: Katherine, tell me something. Before I told you about our interview – before I told you what he said about Lewis, what was your impression of him?

KATHERINE: That's a silly question. I was only with him a few minutes. How could I possibly …

ROBERT: Come off it! You always make snap decisions about people, you know that! What was your impression of Carl May?

KATHERINE: I should think he's pretty shrewd; and pretty ruthless, too, when he wants to be.

ROBERT: Can you see what Eve sees in him?

KATHERINE: Yes; I can. He's an attractive man; probably very good company. Pretty generous too, I should imagine.

ROBERT: M'm.

KATHERINE: He reminded me of someone, Robert – you'll never guess who.

ROBERT: Who?

KATHERINE: He reminded me of Lewis.

ROBERT: (*Surprised*) Lewis? (*Thoughtfully*) By God, Katherine – I can see what you mean …

In the background: sound of a car pulling into the kerb.

KATHERINE: Is this your car?

ROBERT: (*His thoughts elsewhere*) What? Oh, yes. (*Opens car door*) Jump in, Katherine.

KATHERINE: Wait a minute! Who's that man over there – getting out of that car?

ROBERT: Where? Oh, it's Eric!

DALY: (*Calling from background*) Robert! I'll be with you in a minute.

KATHERINE: I seem to know his face …

ROBERT: He's a colleague of mine – Eric Daly. I think you've met him, Katherine.

KATHERINE: Yes, of course! I thought I recognised him.

DALY: (*Approaching*) Hello, Robert! It looks as if I've just caught you. Good evening, Mrs Hauptmann.

KATHERINE: Good evening, Inspector.

ROBERT: We're just about to drive over to Mrs Bristol's. Did you want me, Eric?

DALY: Yes, I did. I – I wanted to have a talk with you.

ROBERT: (*Hesitating*) Well …

KATHERINE: I can easily pick up a taxi, Robert. You can meet me at Eve's later.

ROBERT: No, there's no need for that, Katherine.

DALY: May I make a suggestion, Mrs Hauptmann?

KATHERINE: Yes, of course.

DALY: Robert, drop Mrs Hauptmann at your sister-in- law's and then meet me at the Royal Gate Hotel in … What time is it now? … At seven o'clock.

111

ROBERT: Yes, all right, Eric. But why the Royal Gate Hotel?

DALY: There's someone there I particularly want you to meet. See you later, Robert.

ROBERT: I'll be there, Eric. Seven o'clock.

DALY: Goodbye, Mrs Hauptmann. I expect we shall meet again.

KATHERINE: Yes, I expect so. Goodbye, Inspector.

ROBERT: Jump in, Katherine.

Car door closes. Sound of car starting.
Fade on car driving away.

Fade in: dance music.
Fade Music to background.

ROBERT: Eric, I'm sorry I'm late. I got caught in a traffic jam at Marble Arch.

DALY: That's all right. How's Mrs Bristol?

ROBERT: She's not at all bad, considering. The doctor's been two or three times and he seems quite pleased with her.

DALY: Oh, good. Is she up?

ROBERT: Yes; and she's talking of going back to work tomorrow. But I doubt whether she'll make it. Well – what's your news?

DALY: First: what would you like to drink?

ROBERT: I'll have a lager.

DALY: A lager and a gin and tonic, please.

WAITER: Yes, sir.

DALY: I talked to Berry Nelson this morning. He still says he knows nothing about the belt and can't understand what it was doing in his dressing room.

ROBERT: Yes, I know. Carl May came to see me this evening; he told me you'd seen Berry.

112

DALY: Carl May? He's Berry's manager.

ROBERT: That's right.

DALY: But why should Carl May pay you a visit?

ROBERT: (*Interrupting him*) I'll tell you about May later. Give me your news first. Why are we meeting here? Who is it you want me to see?

DALY: May I tell the story in my own, slow, lugubrious way?

ROBERT: (*Laughing*) Yes, go on, Eric, if you insist.

DALY: I insist. Well, after I'd seen Berry Nelson – and his wife, by the way …

ROBERT: His wife?

DALY: Yes, she was at the hospital and we had quite a little chat. She's separated from Berry but she's obviously still in love with the little bastard. Anyway, after I'd seen Nelson, I went back to the office and there was a note on my desk from Sergeant Thornton. Thornton's been making inquiries about various people who used to work for your sister-in-law.

ROBERT: At La Boutique?

DALY: Yes. Mrs Bristol's had several assistants and a girl called Simone Duprez was with her for almost a year.

ROBERT: I remember Simone. She's a Belgian; a brunette, very good looking.

DALY: That's right. She left La Boutique about six months ago and she's now an air hostess with International Airlines. They have their headquarters in this hotel.

ROBERT: Go on, Eric.

DALY: Thornton and I interviewed Simone this afternoon and there's not the slightest doubt that she was puzzled – very puzzled – by certain things that happened whilst she was working at La Boutique.

ROBERT: What sort of thing?

DALY: Well – for instance: one morning, apparently, she arrived at the shop at about … Wait a minute! Here she is! She'll tell you all about it herself. (*A slight pause*) Good evening, Miss Duprez …

SIMONE: Good evening, Inspector.

DALY: This is Superintendent Bristol …

SIMONE: How do you do? I think we've met before …

ROBERT: Yes, we have. Do sit down.

SIMONE: Thank you.

ROBERT: Can I get you a drink, Miss Duprez?

SIMONE: No, not for me, thank you.

DALY: Will you have a cigarette?

SIMONE: No, I don't think I will, thank you, Inspector. I'm trying to cut down on them. (*A moment*) I was sorry to … read about … your brother, Mr Bristol.

ROBERT: Yes, well … Miss Duprez, Inspector Daly tells me that when you were working at La Boutique you were a little curious about certain things that happened there.

SIMONE: Yes, I was, but … (*Slightly embarrassed*) I don't really think it's of any importance. Eve – Mrs Bristol – was frightfully kind to me and I should hate to think that anything I said might … get her into trouble.

ROBERT: (*With a little laugh*) If it's not important, it's not going to get anyone into trouble.

DALY: Please, Miss Duprez, just tell the Superintendent what you told me this afternoon.

SIMONE: My father has a dress shop in Brussels and just over a year ago I applied for a job at La Boutique. I wanted to learn the language and I was crazy

114

to work in London. For the first two or three months I enjoyed it immensely; Mrs Bristol was terribly kind to me, and Miss Mortimer – well, I managed to keep on the right side of her. And then certain things happened which I just couldn't understand.

ROBERT: What sort of things?

SIMONE: Well – we used to leave the shop at about six o'clock in the evening, sometimes a little later. Everything was put away before we left; the dresses on hangers; the cupboards closed; everything nice and tidy. But sometimes when I arrived at the shop the next morning, the dresses would be out again. It was just as if the shop had been open during the night.

ROBERT: Did this happen very often?

SIMONE: Perhaps … half a dozen times.

ROBERT: Did you ever comment on it?

SIMONE: Yes, I did. On one occasion I asked Miss Mortimer what was going on and she simply told me to mind my own business. Later she apologised for being rude and said they'd been stocktaking. She didn't sound very convincing.

ROBERT: You don't think she was telling the truth, in fact?

SIMONE: No, I'm afraid I don't.

ROBERT: Then what's your explanation? What do you think happened?

SIMONE: I – I just don't know.

ROBERT: Well, if you had to hazard a guess, what would you say?

SIMONE: (*Hesitant*) I've already told you. It was just as if the shop had been open during the night.

ROBERT: (*Thoughtfully*) I see.

DALY: Now tell him about the phone call, Miss Duprez.

SIMONE: About two or three days before I left La Boutique there was a phone call from San Francisco. Eve was away, I think she had the flu or something, and it so happened that Miss Mortimer wasn't in the shop either.

ROBERT: Go on …

SIMONE: I took the call and a man said, "This is Rolf Winter … Our contact will be calling on Thursday and for God's sake make sure she gets the right belt this time."

ROBERT: "Our contact will be calling on Thursday and for God's sake make sure she gets the right belt this time"?

SIMONE: Yes.

ROBERT: And what did you say?

SIMONE: I said: "I'm sorry, Mrs Bristol's away and I don't know what you're talking about."

ROBERT: And then?

SIMONE: He just said, "Oh, that isn't Mrs Bristol speaking then?" and rang off. When Miss Mortimer returned, I told her about the call, and she said she just couldn't understand it. She said she'd never heard of anyone called Winter.

ROBERT: Did you speak to Eve about it?

SIMONE: No.

ROBERT: Why not?

SIMONE: Two days later I left La Boutique and joined International Airways. I had other things to think about.

ROBERT: Yes, I'm sure.

SIMONE: Inspector – Mr Bristol – will you excuse me? I'm leaving for Hong Kong tomorrow morning and I've an awful lot to do.

ROBERT: Yes, of course. And thank you for your help, Miss Duprez.

SIMONE: Not at all …

DALY: Goodbye …

SIMONE: Goodbye, Inspector. Give my regards to Sergeant Thornton.

A pause.

DALY: Do you believe her?

ROBERT: Yes, I do. Completely.

DALY: So do I. Well – where do we go from here, Robert?

ROBERT: I know where I'm going. I'm going to talk to my sister-in-law!

Fade in Music.

Fade down Music.

Fade in: doorbell ringing. Door opens.

PEARL: (*Surprised*) Oh, hello, Robert!

ROBERT: (*Surprised*) Oh, hello – Pearl!

PEARL: (*Laughing*) Come along in! You know, if you'd be happier with "Miss Mortimer", don't let's stand on ceremony. (*Closes the door*)

ROBERT: Is my sister still here?

PEARL: Yes; she's in the kitchen helping me to get dinner ready. Have you eaten?

ROBERT: Well …

PEARL: Good! It'll be ready in ten minutes.

They enter the lounge.

ROBERT: Where's Eve?

PEARL: She's in the bedroom, on the phone, she'll be out in a minute.

ROBERT: How is she?

PEARL: Oh – she's very much better.

Bedroom door opens.

117

EVE: Is that you, Robert?

ROBERT: Oh, hello, Eve!

KATHERINE: (*Calling from kitchen*) Miss Mortimer – Pearl! Help! Everything's boiling over!

PEARL: (*Amused*) That's little sister. You'd think she was married to a plumber instead of a hotelier. She can't even boil an egg.

EVE: I'll give you a hand!

PEARL: No, no, you stay where you are! And pour that brother-in-law of yours a large whisky and soda, he looks as if he can use it.

Kitchen door opens and closes.

ROBERT: I can't imagine what she's like in her own flat.

EVE: Well – you know Pearl.

ROBERT: That's just it – I don't know her.

EVE: What do you mean?

ROBERT: May I have the whisky and soda?

EVE: Yes, of course. Help yourself, Robert.

ROBERT: (*Mixing drink*) Would you like one?

EVE: No; I don't think so, thanks. I've just taken one of those tablets, I'd better be careful.

ROBERT: You look very much better.

EVE: Yes, I feel it.

ROBERT: Good. Skoal! (*Drinks; then:*) Eve, when you told me about the letter – the photograph – that Lewis gave you, I asked you if you'd ever heard of the man whose name was on the envelope.

EVE: Rolf … Winter?

ROBERT: That's right. You said you hadn't.

EVE: Well – I hadn't.

ROBERT: Then why should he telephone you, if you'd never heard of him?

EVE: (*Apparently puzzled*) What do you mean? What are you talking about?

ROBERT: I'm talking about the phone call from San Francisco.

EVE: What telephone call? I've never had a phone call from San Francisco in my life.

ROBERT: It came through to the shop, you were out, so Miss Duprez took it.

EVE: When was this?

ROBERT: About six months ago; just before Miss Duprez left you.

A pause.

EVE: You've seen Simone, I take it?

ROBERT: Yes.

EVE: When?

ROBERT: Tonight. Tell me about the phone call. What did Rolf Winter mean when he said, "Our contact will be calling for the belt – make sure she gets the right one this time"?

EVE: I'm sorry, I don't know what you're talking about, Robert. I just don't know anything about this.

ROBERT: Eve, I don't want to upset you, that's the last thing I want to do; but I've got to get to the bottom of this! You've got to tell me about that phone call; you've got to tell me about Rolf Winter!

EVE: I've told you the truth! I know nothing about this phone call and I'd never heard of Rolf Winter until I saw his name on that envelope.

ROBERT: All right, Eve, let's forget the …

EVE: You don't believe me, do you?

ROBERT: Let's forget the phone call for the moment. Now would you mind explaining something else to me?

Miss Duprez, who seems to me to be a pretty reliable sort of person, told me that …

PEARL: (*From kitchen doorway*) Pretty's the word! Reliable? That's open to question, I'm afraid.

EVE: (*Quietly*) Robert's been talking to Simone.

PEARL: (*Coming into the room*) Yes, so I gather. Is this a family quarrel or may anyone join in?

ROBERT: (*Irritated by Pearl's manner*) It isn't a quarrel at all. I'm just asking some questions; if you know the answers, okay – let's have them.

PEARL: In what capacity are you asking the questions, Mr Bristol? As a Police Superintendent or as a friend?

ROBERT: Let's say as a very friendly Police Superintendent, Miss Mortimer.

EVE: Oh, for God's sake! Come off it, Pearl – Robert …

PEARL: What is it you want to know?

EVE: Simone told Robert that just before she left La Boutique there was a phone call for me from San Francisco; from a man called Rolf Winter.

PEARL: This is news to me. Are you supposed to have taken the call?

ROBERT: No. Eve was away with the flu and Miss Duprez took it.

PEARL: If it came through to the shop, why didn't I take it?

ROBERT: Apparently you were out at the time.

PEARL: Oh, I see. (*With sarcasm*) Eve was away and I was out, so Miss Duprez took this very important call from San Francisco.

ROBERT: (*Irritated*) I didn't say it was important.

PEARL: Well, if it isn't important what the devil are you worried about?

ROBERT: (*Holding his temper*) You know nothing about the call?

PEARL: Nothing. But while we're talking about Miss Duprez, may I put you in the picture?

ROBERT: Go on …

PEARL: She's a very good-looking girl; she has great charm; she knows how to wear clothes.

ROBERT: I've seen her, I know what she looks like!

PEARL: But she's completely and utterly unreliable …

EVE: Now, Pearl, wait a minute! I wouldn't say that …

PEARL: I know you wouldn't, Eve, because you never say an unkind thing about anyone …

EVE: Oh, nonsense!

PEARL: It's true, darling.

ROBERT: How was she unreliable?

PEARL: What?

ROBERT: I said: "How was she unreliable?"

PEARL: Well – to give you an example – when we're busy at the shop, really busy, we have dresses and coats strewn all over the place. The shop looks as if a bomb's just hit it. This means, at the end of the day, when the shop's closed, we have to stay behind and tidy up – or come in early the next morning. Do you think dear Simone used to stay behind, or come in early? Not Pygmalion likely! At night there was always some long-haired character hovering in the background, and in the morning … (*Assuming Simone's accent*) "I'm so sorry, Mrs Bristol, I just don't know what happened to me this morning, I'm afraid I overslept."

ROBERT: Is this true, Eve?

EVE: I'm very fond of Simone, I like her enormously, I …

121

PEARL:	Oh, for God's sake, Eve! Am I telling the truth or am I not telling the truth?
EVE:	Well – she was awfully good with customers, Pearl.
PEARL:	I didn't say she wasn't! She was marvellous in some ways. I admit it! (*To Robert*) If a man walked in with his wife – he'd had it! His cheque book was out, and he was signing on the dotted line, before his wife tried on a blessed thing! But nevertheless, she was lazy and more often than not utterly unreliable.

Door opens.

KATHERINE:	(*Urgently*) Pearl … Eve … Someone get hold of these plates! Quickly! They're very hot …
PEARL:	(*Quickly*) It's all right, I've got them!
EVE:	Let me give you a hand!
PEARL:	No, no, it's all right! Everything's under control.
KATHERINE:	Hello, Robert!
ROBERT:	(*His thoughts elsewhere*) Oh, hello, Katherine.
PEARL:	You sit down, Mrs Hauptmann. I'll see to things.
KATHERINE:	The sooner I get back home the better! Thank heavens we live in a hotel! If we didn't I'm afraid poor old Freddie would starve.
PEARL:	(*Going into the kitchen*) You're spoiled, that's your trouble.
EVE:	We shall need another chair, Robert. There's one in the hall.
ROBERT:	What? Oh, yes! I'll get it …
EVE:	(*Start Fade*) Would you like a drink before dinner, Katherine?
KATHERINE:	May I have a glass of sherry?

EVE: Of course …

Complete Fade.

Fade in; hall clock chiming. Eight o'clock.
Fade on chimes.
A knock: door opens.

MRS WEBB: Good morning, sir.

ROBERT: (*In bed; yawning*) Oh, good morning, Mrs
                Webb.

MRS WEBB: I've brought you a cup of tea, sir.

ROBERT: Oh, thank you. What time is it?

MRS WEBB: It's just gone eight.

ROBERT: Heavens, I'm late this morning!

MRS WEBB: (*Putting tray down*) I don't know about that,
                dearie. You're still supposed to be on holiday,
                remember.

ROBERT: I'm glad you said "remember". Is my sister
                awake?

MRS WEBB: Yes. I'm just running her bath. Here's the
                morning papers.

ROBERT: Thank you.

MRS WEBB: There's a report of the Inquest.

ROBERT: I expect there is. (*Dismissing her*) Thank you,
                Mrs Webb.

MRS WEBB: The funeral's this afternoon then?

ROBERT: Yes. This afternoon. Two o'clock.

MRS WEBB: Well – it's a nice day for it. I always think a
                funeral's terrible when it rains. Will you be
                wanting a meal this afternoon, sir?

ROBERT: A meal?

MRS WEBB: Yes.

ROBERT: No; why on earth should I want … Oh, I see
                what you mean. No, nothing like that, Mrs
                Webb. Mrs Hauptmann will be coming back

	to the flat to change, that's all – then I'm running her to the airport. She's flying home this afternoon.
MRS WEBB:	I'll have a nice cup of tea ready for her.
ROBERT:	Yes, you do that, Mrs Webb. I'm sure she'd appreciate it.

Telephone rings.

MRS WEBB:	Shall I take it, sir?
ROBERT:	No, I'll get it. (*Leans over and lifts receiver*) Hello?
ELKA:	(*On the other end*) Hello? Who is that, please?
ROBERT:	Who is it you want?
ELKA:	I – I'd like to speak to Superintendent Bristol.
ROBERT:	I'm Robert Bristol. Who is it speaking?
ELKA:	Mr Bristol, you don't know me – we've never met – but ... I'm Elka Nelson.
ROBERT:	Elka Nels ... Oh, good morning, Mrs Nelson. What can I do for you?
ELKA:	I was wondering if it would be possible, perhaps ... for us to meet sometime?
ROBERT:	I don't see why not, Mrs Nelson. But why not get in touch with Inspector Daly? He's the one making enquiries about what happened to your husband.
ELKA:	(*Disappointed*) Very well. If you think it would be better for me to see Inspector Daly, then of course ...
ROBERT:	(*Curious*) No, no, that's all right. I'll see you, Mrs Nelson, if you'd prefer it. When would you like to meet?
ELKA:	Could you make it this afternoon?
ROBERT:	No, that's not possible. I could meet you this evening though.

ELKA: About half past six?

ROBERT: Yes, I could manage that.

ELKA: I work at a little café on the King's Road. It's called The Sun Tan.

ROBERT: (*Surprised*) Do you want me to come to the café?

ELKA: Yes, I think so. It's very quiet there. Easy to talk. If you get there first just tell Oscar, he's the proprietor, I'm expecting you.

ROBERT: All right – but why not come here? It's quiet here, too, Mrs Nelson.

ELKA: Yes, I know, but – it's not unusual for me to go to the café. It's just routine.

ROBERT: I see. Very well. I'll be there. The Sun Tan. King's Road. Half past six …

Fade in Music.

Fade Music.

Fade in: typewriter. Typing stops as door opens.

DALY: Any luck, Hilda? Have you located him?

HILDA: No. But I've just spoken to his housekeeper. Apparently as soon as the funeral was over, he drove his sister out to London Airport.

DALY: Yes, but that must have been about half past two. What time is it now?

HILDA: It feels like midnight. (*Taking document from typewriter*) This blasted report! It's a quarter past five …

DALY: Did Mrs Webb say whether she was expecting him back or not?

HILDA: No. She said she didn't know what he was doing tonight, but she thinks he has an appointment somewhere at half past six.

DALY: That's a great help! (*Door opens*) All right, Hilda, I think we'd better forget … Robert!

125

ROBERT: Hello, Eric …

DALY: I've been trying to get in touch with you, old boy! I phoned your flat three times, and Mrs Webb …

ROBERT: (*Tired; faintly irritated*) Yes, I know. I got the message. That's why I'm here.

DALY: (*Kindly*) Would you like a cup of tea?

ROBERT: Good grief, no! I'm up to here in tea! What is it, Eric? What's happened? Why do you want to see me?

DALY: You can go, Hilda. You can finish that tomorrow morning.

HILDA: Are you kidding? It'll take a week to finish off this epic.

DALY: Chief-Superintendent Tomlinson, I suppose?

HILDA: You said it, sir – not me.

ROBERT: What's the matter with that man? He's not a detective, he's a ruddy author!

Hilda laughs as she goes out, closing the door behind her.

DALY: (*Quietly*) I've got some news, Robert.

ROBERT: Well?

DALY: You know you told me to check on Winter, to find out what I could about him?

ROBERT: Yes.

DALY: Well, yesterday afternoon I decided that I was getting nowhere, so I took the bull by the horns and cabled Sam Sutton. Do you remember Sam Sutton?

ROBERT: He's with the F.B.I.; he worked with you on the Bermuda case.

DALY: That's right. Sam became a good friend of mine and … Anyway, he phoned me this morning. Winter's a millionaire. He's supposed to have made his money out of legitimate business but …

126

ROBERT: What do you mean – <u>supposed</u> to have made his money out of legitimate business?

DALY: To put it bluntly. The F.B.I. don't like him. They think his business activities and his outward appearance of respectability are just a cover. Apparently in 1965 he was questioned by the Federal Bureau of Narcotics. They had a tip-off from the Mexican authorities and the police finally picked him up in San Diego.

ROBERT: The Federal Bureau of Narcotics? You mean – he's peddling dope?

DALY: The F.B.I. think so, but they just can't pin anything on him. They suspect he controls the whole network in California.

ROBERT: Is that what your friend Sam Sutton told you?

DALY: Yes.

ROBERT: This is interesting. Really interesting, Eric. (*Thoughtfully*) At last things are beginning to add up...

DALY: I'm glad you think so. Your arithmetic must be better than mine.

ROBERT: (*Suddenly*) Eric, you've seen Berry Nelson – you've talked to him at the hospital?

DALY: Yes.

ROBERT: Is he on drugs? Is he an addict?

DALY: (*Surprised by the question*) Berry? Why, no ... At least ... I never thought about it. There's a hell of a lot of it going on with these pop singers, of course, but ... No; I saw the doctor, surely to God he'd have told me if there'd been anything like that.

ROBERT: Have another word with the hospital and I'll talk to Mrs Nelson about it.

DALY: Mrs Nelson?

127

ROBERT: Yes. She phoned me this morning and said she wanted to see me. I'm meeting her at a café on the King's Road at half past six.

DALY: That'll be The Sun Tan.

ROBERT: That's right.

DALY: She works there. Look Robert – I don't want to step out of line, but …

ROBERT: Say what you think Eric. I'm the one that's stepping out of line. Officially, I'm still on leave.

DALY: Nonsense! I was just going to say – well, don't you think it might be a good idea if someone went with you to the café? One of the girls, perhaps? Hilda, or Janet, or …

ROBERT: I'd rather go on my own, Eric. But this is your case. If you feel …

DALY: No; no, we'll play it your way, Robert. But we'll keep an eye on the place anyway …

ROBERT: What's Mrs Nelson like? Describe her to me.

DALY: (*Start Fade*) She's about twenty-six. Quite tall, about five foot eight, I should think. She was born in Munich and she first came over here in 1964 …

Complete Fade.

Fade in: traffic noises. Police car draws into the kerb.

DALY: (*In car*) We'll drop you here, we don't want to park too near the café.

ROBERT: (*In car; opening door*) Right! I'll see you later, Eric.

COLMAN: The café's about fifty yards down on the right-hand side, sir.

ROBERT: I can see it, Colman. There's an awning outside.

THORNTON: (*In car*) No, that's a supermarket. The Sun Tan's just a bit further on.

128

ROBERT: I'll find it, Thornton.

Car door opens and closes. Fade up traffic noises.
Fade.

Café door opens and closes.
Traffic noises in distant background.

OSCAR: (*Tired; old*) Good evening, sir.

ROBERT: Good evening.

OSCAR: Quite pleasant out this evening.

ROBERT: Yes, it is.

OSCAR: Shall I take your coat, sir?

ROBERT: No, that's all right. May I have the table in the
              window?

OSCAR: Please. You've plenty to choose from. We're
              never busy at this time of day. But excuse me
              – are you the gentleman Elka – Mrs
              Nelson's expecting?

ROBERT: Yes, I am.

OSCAR: Then sit over here, sir. In the alcove. You'll
              be able to talk better. Elka should be here any
              minute now. It's half past six; she's very
              punctual as a rule.

ROBERT: How long has Mrs Nelson been working for
              you?

OSCAR: Only three weeks. She's very nice; very
              helpful. Can't do too much for us … Let me
              pull the table out, sir … The customers like
              her, and that's everything. Of course, she
              shouldn't have to work at all, you know. That
              husband of hers is lousy with money.

ROBERT: You mean our little heart-throb – Hardy?

OSCAR: That's right, but she calls him Berry. I know
              what I'd call him. He came here one night.
              Showing off; poncing around. I said to him,

"Are you sure you can get your head through the door, young man?" Would you like a cup of coffee while you're waiting, sir?

ROBERT: Thank you.

Fade in - traffic noises.

Fade to background.

THORNTON: ...I don't agree with you, Inspector. In my opinion these kids, these pop singers like Hardy Nelson, just don't have any problems.

DALY: He had problems the other night when he was beaten up.

THORNTON: Yes, I know, but – I mean the sort of problems we have.

COLMAN: I think the Sergeant's right, sir. Now you take my Missis. Last week she paid forty-five quid for a washing machine. She'd been saving up for this blasted washing machine for over ... (*Stops*) What is it?

DALY: There she is – there's Mrs Nelson.

THORNTON: Where?

DALY: She's standing near the tobacconist's – just about to cross the road ...

THORNTON: In the blue coat?

DALY: That's right.

THORNTON: Not bad, eh, Colman? How would you like that and five hundred a week? And the Inspector says the little basket's got problems!

COLMAN: (*Seriously; watching Elka*) Wait a minute! Who's that chap ...?

THORNTON: Where?

DALY: There's someone talking to her ...

THORNTON: (*A moment*) Yes ... Where did he come from?

130

DALY: He must have been in one of the doorways.

THORNTON: Was he waiting for her?

DALY: I don't know.

COLMAN: He's a tourist, you can tell by his camera. He's just asking her the way somewhere, that's all.

THORNTON: Yes, I think you're right.

DALY: I'm not sure about this.

A pause.

THORNTON: He's taking a devil of a time if he's just asking her the way.

DALY: Yes; that's what I think – and he seems to be doing all the talking.

Sound of sports car racing past.

COLMAN: Well, if you like, sir, we can drive past and ... (*Suddenly; staggered*) Look at those two men! In that sports car ...

THORNTON: One of them's got a gun!

DALY: What the hell are they doing?

Sound of gun shots.

COLMAN: My God!

THORNTON: She's been hit!

DALY: He shot her!

THORNTON: And the man! Look – he's on the pavement!

DALY: They've both been hit!

Fade up; traffic noises; excited voices.

Sports car racing away.

Colman presses starter. Police car starts.

COLMAN: Did you get the number?

DALY: To hell with the number! After them, Colman!

Fade up; police car racing in pursuit of sports car.

Fade.

Fade in: Crowd on pavement; excited voices; Robert pushing his way through the mob.

ROBERT: Excuse me … Please let me through. I'm a police officer … Excuse me! Will you please make way …

ELKA: (*In pain*) Are – Are you a doctor?

FELSTON: Yes; now don't worry, my dear …

ELKA: Am I … going to be all right?

FELSTON: Yes; I'll be able to give you an injection in a few minutes, then you won't feel a thing.

ELKA: Please … tell my husband that … (*In obvious pain*)

FELSTON: Don't talk, my dear … We'll get in touch with your husband … There's absolutely nothing to worry about …

ROBERT: Doctor … I'm Superintendent Bristol.

FELSTON: Felston's my name. I was in the tobacconist's when I heard the shots.

ROBERT: (*Aside*) Is she going to be all right?

FELSTON: Yes; she was lucky – it's just a flesh wound so far as I can tell. But she's frightened, devilishly frightened poor girl, so I'm going to give her a sedative.

ROBERT: And the man?

FELSTON: That's a different story, I'm afraid. He's dead. Do you know him, by any chance?

ROBERT: (*A moment*) Yes, I know him.

Fade up background noises and sound of approaching ambulance.

Fade.

Fade in: police car racing along the Embankment. Siren blaring.

Fade.

Fade in; sports car racing along the Embankment.

Police siren can be heard in the distant background.

OWEN: (*Worried*) He's still with us … You haven't shaken him, Terry.

NEWTON:(*Agitated*) I know! Do you think I'm deaf or something …

OWEN: This is one for the book, man. I didn't expect this …

NEWTON:No; neither did I … Something went wrong …

OWEN: What was the police car doing there? Were they watching the café?

NEWTON:God knows!

OWEN: Step on it, Terry!

NEWTON:What d'you mean – step on it! I've already got my flaming foot through the …

OWEN: (*Suddenly, alarmed*) Keep your eyes on the road, man! (*Relieved*) Phew! For God's sake …

NEWTON:All right! All right! I know what I'm doing!

OWEN: Where the hell are we making for?

NEWTON:Chelsea Bridge … As soon as we get the other side of the river we'll ditch the car and … Hell – more bloody lights!

OWEN: Steady now! Watch it, man – it's on red.

NEWTON:Red! Green! What the hell's the difference?

Sound of lorry approaching crossroads.

OWEN: You'll know the difference if … (*Shouting*) There's a lorry coming! Look out! Terry, for God's sake!

Sound of lorry; horn blowing. Screeching of brakes. The sports car hits the lorry head on.

Fade in; police car racing up, sirens blaring. Police car brakes to a standstill.

Fade in Music.

Fade down Music.
Telephone ringing.
Ringing stops as receiver is lifted.

VIRGINIA: Hello?
PORTER: (*On the other end*) Mrs Winter?
VIRGINIA: Yes, speaking.
PORTER: This is the hall porter, madam. Sorry to disturb you but Superintendent Bristol would like to see you. He's downstairs in the vestibule.
VIRGINIA: I'm sorry, I can't see anyone at the moment. Tell him I'm … (*A moment; changing her mind*) Very well. Ask him to wait. I'll come down. (*Replaces receiver*)

Fade.

Fade in: knock on a door.
VIRGINIA: (*Calling*) Come in!
Door opens.
ROBERT: Mrs Winter …
VIRGINIA: (*Annoyed*) Mr Bristol, I told the porter I'd see you downstairs! I'm very sorry but I just can't …
ROBERT: (*Interrupting her*) Yes, I know you did. I won't keep you a moment. (*Closes door.*)
VIRGINIA: (*Nervous; uncertain of herself*) What is it you want?
ROBERT: I'm afraid I've got some very bad news for you, Mrs Winter.
VIRGINIA: Bad news?
ROBERT: (*A moment*) Your husband's dead. He was killed – shot – just over an hour ago.
VIRGINIA: (*Stunned*) Dead? He's …dead?

ROBERT: Yes, I'm afraid so.

VIRGINIA: (*Still hardly believing him*) Are you sure?

ROBERT: Yes, I'm quite sure.

VIRGINIA: Rolf Winter ... is ... dead?

ROBERT: Yes.

Suddenly, to Robert's astonishment, Virginia starts laughing.

VIRGINIA: Bad news, did you say? Bad news? ...

Virginia continues laughing, her laughter growing until it seems almost uncontrollable; very near hysteria.

End of Part Four

Part Five

ROBERT: I'm afraid I've got some very bad news for
            you, Mrs Winter.
VIRGINIA: Bad news?
ROBERT: (*A moment*) Your husband's dead. He was
            killed – shot – just over an hour ago.
VIRGINIA: (*Stunned*) Dead? He's ...dead?
ROBERT: Yes, I'm afraid so.
VIRGINIA: (*Still hardly believing him*) Are you sure?
ROBERT: Yes, I'm quite sure.
VIRGINIA: Rolf Winter ... is ... dead?
ROBERT: Yes.

Suddenly, to Robert's astonishment, Virginia starts laughing.

VIRGINIA: Bad news, did you say? Bad news? ...

*Virginia continues laughing, her laughter growing until it
seems almost uncontrollable; very near hysteria.*

ROBERT: Mrs Winter, stop it! Stop it!

Robert hits her across the face.

VIRGINIA: Oh! ... (*Catching her breath*) Oh ...
ROBERT: Now stop it! (*A pause*) Are you all right?
VIRGINIA: Yes, I ... I ...
ROBERT: (*Concerned*) Are you sure?
VIRGINIA: Yes, I'm all right now.
ROBERT: I'm sorry I had to do that. Did I hurt you?
VIRGINIA: No ... No, you didn't hurt me, Mr Bristol.
ROBERT: Let me get you a drink.
VIRGINIA: I don't drink, I ... (*Hesitates*) Yes, I will have
            one. Thank you. The cabinet's over there ...
ROBERT: Do you think I might have a Scotch?
VIRGINIA: Yes, of course. Please ...
ROBERT: I certainly feel I could use one, right now!

A pause. Robert mixes drinks.

VIRGINIA: Tell me: what happened tonight? What
            happened to Rolf?

ROBERT:	(*Still mixing drinks*) I'd arranged to meet a girl called Elka Nelson. She's married to Hardy Nelson, the pop singer. We were supposed to meet in a café on the King's Road, Chelsea. On the way to the café your husband stopped Mrs Nelson and started talking to her. They were standing on the pavement talking when two men suddenly appeared in a sports car. One of the men had a gun. He shot your husband.
VIRGINIA:	And Mrs Nelson?
ROBERT:	She was injured.
VIRGINIA:	Seriously?
ROBERT:	No; her leg was grazed, that's all. I doubt whether they'll even keep her in hospital more than twenty-four hours.
VIRGINIA:	What happened to the two men?
ROBERT:	Their car crashed into a lorry on the Embankment. One of them was killed. Here's your drink, Mrs Winter.
VIRGINIA:	Thank you.
A pause.	
ROBERT:	(*After drinking*) Would you like me to go when I've finished this, or would you like to talk to me?
VIRGINIA:	Talk to you?
ROBERT:	About your husband – about Lewis.
VIRGINA:	That's a long story, I'm afraid.
ROBERT:	I'm in no hurry, Mrs Winter. I've got all the time in the world. Believe it or not, I'm even supposed to be on holiday.
VIRGINIA:	What – what is it you want to know?

ROBERT: Did you deliberately get friendly with my brother that night, at the party? Was it all prearranged – part of a plan?

VIRGINIA: Yes.

A pause.

ROBERT: Well – are you going to tell me about it, Mrs Winter?

VIRGINIA: (*Tensely*) Oh, please, please don't call me Mrs Winter. Yes, I'll tell you about it; I'll tell you all about Lewis and ... what happened in San Francisco ...

Fade in Music.
Fade Music.

Fade in: typewriter. Door opens.

DALY: Good morning, Hilda.

HILDA: Good morning, sir.

DALY: How are you this morning?

HILDA: Oh, I'm all right. Still working on the epic. The Superintendent's in your office.

DALY: Yes, I know. Has Mrs Bristol arrived yet?

HILDA: She's been and gone. She left about ten minutes ago.

DALY: (*Surprised*) Oh ...

HILDA: And there's a Mr Carl May downstairs. He says he hasn't got an appointment but he'd very much like to see you.

DALY: All right. Have him come up.

Hilda picks up telephone and dials.

Door of inner office opens and closes.

DALY: Good morning, Robert.

ROBERT: (*Folding up newspaper*) Hello, Eric ...

DALY: Sorry I'm late. I've been in the lab talking to O'Hara.

141

ROBERT: Oh – what's he have to say?

DALY: He's examined the belt we found in Nelson's dressing room. He says the belt's okay but the buckle's hollow and at some time or other it's been used as a container. He found traces of heroin in it.

ROBERT: I see.

DALY: O'Hara's also of the opinion that there are quite a few of these belts in existence and the one we found on Lewis wasn't necessarily the one Mrs Bristol gave you. Which, if it's true, puts us back to square one. In other words, what happened to the belt you had? You swore you'd packed it.

ROBERT: I did pack it.

DALY: Then what's the answer?

ROBERT: The answer, curiously enough, and you won't believe me, Eric, is a cup of coffee.

DALY: A cup of coffee?

ROBERT: (*Laughing*) Yes, and don't ask me to explain what I mean, old boy, because I'm not going to! (*Suddenly; changing the subject*) I've already seen Eve – Mrs Bristol. She was early and there was no point in her hanging around once she'd seen the photographs. You were right. It was Newton and Owen that broke into her flat. She identified both of them.

DALY: Well, Owen won't talk, I'm afraid. Not at the moment, at any rate. I spent half an hour with him last night.

ROBERT: Not at the moment? Does that mean you think he will talk?

DALY: I think he could be persuaded, but I'm not sure. He was certainly very rattled when I told him

> Newton had been killed and the lorry driver was still unconscious.

ROBERT: How the devil Owen escaped injury, I shall never understand.

DALY: The incredible thing is, he hasn't a scratch on him – not a mark. And the car was a write-off. A complete write-off.

Door opens.

HILDA: Mr May's here, sir.

ROBERT: (*Surprised*) Carl May?

DALY: Yes – apparently he wants to see me. I'll talk to him in the other office, if you like, Robert.

ROBERT: No, no, let's have him in.

DALY: All right, Hilda. (*To Robert*) I haven't the slightest idea what he wants to see me about.

ROBERT: I can guess. Hardy Nelson left the hospital last night.

DALY: You mean – he was discharged?

ROBERT: He discharged himself. As soon as he heard what has happened to his wife he just walked out.

HILDA: Mr May, sir.

DALY: Come in, Mr May. I'm Chief-Inspector Daly. I think you've met the Superintendent.

CARL: (*Faintly surprised to see Robert*) Yes. Yes, indeed. Good morning.

ROBERT: Good morning.

DALY: What can I do for you, sir?

CARL: I don't know that you can do anything for me, Inspector, but – I'm extremely worried about a friend of mine.

ROBERT: Hardy Nelson?

CARL: Yes. I take it you've heard about him; you know what's happened?

ROBERT: He's left hospital.

143

CARL: That's right; he's discharged himself. Simply walked out – late last night. I've been trying to find him ever since.

DALY: Isn't he at home?

CARL: (*Obviously worried; on edge*) No, he isn't. And he isn't at his wife's place either. I've telephoned his friends and been in touch with his relatives. He just seems to have vanished.

DALY: Well, I'm sorry, Mr May, but I fail to see what we can do about it. He's a free agent, over twenty-one, and we haven't a warrant out for him.

CARL: I appreciate that. I was just wondering if, by any chance, he'd been in touch with you.

DALY: No, I'm afraid he hasn't.

CARL: You've heard nothing?

DALY: Nothing at all. But then, there's no reason why we should.

CARL: (*Perturbed*) I thought perhaps he might have contacted you about his wife?

DALY: My word, you are worried, sir.

CARL: Of course I'm worried, Inspector! Berry's a friend of mine, a very good friend, but he's also a property – a very hot property so far as I'm concerned.

ROBERT: I can understand that.

CARL: I've actually got a contract here, in my pocket, offering him fifteen hundred a week.

ROBERT: Fifteen hundred pounds a week!

CARL: Yes, in Las Vegas, and that's without any recording rights. So I don't have to tell you that, right now, I should hate – just hate anything to happen to Hardy Nelson.

ROBERT: Why should anything happen to him? The last time we met you said you felt sure that the

144

beating up he had was unimportant, just a couple of thugs out to steal his wallet.

CARL: Yes, I know. But that was before someone tried to kill his wife.

ROBERT: Now you think there might be more to it?

CARL: Frankly, I don't know what to think. When I read about the attempt on Elka I ... (*A sudden thought*) Incidentally, the man who was killed – Rolf Winter.

ROBERT: Yes?

CARL: (*Puzzled*) Wasn't he the man you mentioned, the man your brother knew? If I remember rightly you said Lewis gave Eve – Mrs Bristol – a letter addressed to Rolf Winter.

Door opens.

ROBERT: Yes, he did. And it was shortly after that, that two men ... (*Stops*)

DALY: Yes – what is it, Hilda?

HILDA: (*Hesitant*) Excuse me, sir. Superintendent Talbot would like to see you.

DALY: (*Surprised*) Superintendent Talbot? ... Right away?

HILDA: Yes, I – I think so, sir. He said it was important.

DALY: All right. (*To Carl*) Excuse me.

Door closes.

DALY: (*Quietly; puzzled*) Hilda, what is this? Talbot's in Manchester.

HILDA: (*Excited*) Yes, I know! Hardy Nelson's on the phone; he wants to talk to you. I didn't want to put him through in case ...

DALY: Good girl! I'll take it in Talbot's office.

Fade.

Fade in: telephone buzzer.

DALY: (*Picking up receiver*) Hello? …

BERRY: (*Agitated; weary*) For God's sake, what's going on?

DALY: Hello, Berry! This is Inspector Daly …

BERRY: At last! I thought you'd emigrated!

DALY: Where are you? Where are you speaking from?

BERRY: I'm in a call-box in Sloane Street. I want to see you, Inspector. Pick me up in a car in twenty minutes.

DALY: Where?

BERRY: In Hyde Park; near the Albert Gate.

DALY: Right! I'll be there.

BERRY: And listen: and I'm not kiddin' mate! Not a word to anyone, you understand?

DALY: I understand, Berry. I get the message. (*Replaces receiver*)

Fade in Music.

Fade Music.

Police car draws into the kerb. Car door opens.

DALY: Jump in, Berry!

BERRY: Just a minute! Who's this character?

ROBERT: I'm Superintendent Bristol …

BERRY: That's right! O' course! Thought I recognised you!

Berry gets into the car. Door closes.

COLMAN: Where to, sir?

BERRY: Drive round the park, mate – and keep going.

ROBERT: (*Amused*) All right, Colman. You've had your orders.

Car drives away.

DALY: How do you feel, Berry?

BERRY: How do I look? I know – terrible! Now listen, I haven't got a lot of time. The wife comes out o'

146

hospital at twelve o'clock and we're flying to Sydney this afternoon.

DALY: To Sydney?

BERRY: That's right.

ROBERT: What is it you want to tell us?

BERRY: Can't you guess? I want to tell you what happened the other night – why I was beaten up.

ROBERT: Go on, Berry.

BERRY: A few days ago, a girl came to see me. She used to be a friend of mine until I discovered ... Well, she's a junky. She told me she needed a hundred quid and said if I gave it to her, she'd tell me something that'd shake me rigid. I was curious, so I coughed up. Man, she shook me.

DALY: What did she tell you, Berry?

BERRY: She said my manager, Carl May, was mixed up in the drug racket; she said he was friendly with a woman who was running a dress shop and they were in it up to their eyes. She gave me a belt, off a dress, and told me to show it to Carl. She said I'd very soon tell, by his reactions, whether she was telling the truth or not.

ROBERT: Did you show him the belt?

BERRY: No, I didn't. I just asked him point blank whether there was any truth in the story.

ROBERT: And what did he say?

BERRY: He just laughed and said it was ridiculous. And like a damn fool I believed him. But it was the next night, the very next night, that I was beaten up. When he saw me in hospital he said, "Berry, it looks to me as if you're getting out of your depth. Little boys shouldn't ask silly questions."

DALY: Go on ...

BERRY: I told my wife what had happened, and she said if I didn't go to the police and tell them the whole story, she would. She said once the police got into Carl May, they'd never believe I wasn't part of the racket, not in a thousand years.

ROBERT: It sounds to me as if you've got a very intelligent wife.

BERRY: Yes, and like a flaming big nit I've only just discovered it. Anyway, we've wiped the slate clean now, thank God – and we're starting all over again.

DALY: In Australia?

BERRY: That's right, cobber. I've got a brother out there. A hairdresser. We're starting up in business together. Hardy Nelson and Associates. Coiffure de dames. London. Paris. New York. We'll make a bloody fortune.

DALY: (*Laughing*) I have a horrible suspicion that you will, Berry.

ROBERT: Berry, tell me: did you ever hear Carl May mention my brother Lewis?

BERRY: Yes; several times. He hated his guts.

ROBERT: Why? Do you know? Was it something to do with his work, his music?

BERRY: (*Laughing*) No, that's what Carl wanted people to think! He was always saying nasty things about your brother; hinting that Lewis didn't really write his music – all that sort of crap. No, I'll tell you the real reason why he didn't like him. Carl's a conceited bastard. He thinks every woman in the world wants to jump into bed with him. Well – several years ago he got friendly with an American girl. She was loaded. Her old man owned half of Texas. Carl was all set for the kill

148

and then – bang, wallop – big brother appeared on the scene.

ROBERT: You mean Lewis?

BERRY: That's right. Do I have to tell you the rest of the story?

ROBERT: (*Pleased*) No – you don't. Thank you, Berry.

BERRY: (*Suddenly*) You can drop me on the corner.

DALY: (*Start Fade*) Wait a minute, Berry. There's still a lot we want to ask you.

BERRY: Then get cracking, mate – get cracking …

Complete Fade.

EVE: (*Fade in: calling*) Pearl! (*Calling*) Pearl!

PEARL: (*Coming from upstairs*) I'm just coming down.

A pause.

EVE: Things are in an awful mess up there, aren't they?

PEARL: Yes, we shall really have to do something about that room one of these days. Are you off to lunch?

EVE: Yes, I'm only just going round the corner. I'll be back by two o'clock.

PEARL: There's no hurry.

EVE: Mrs Lacey's coming for a fitting at two.

PEARL: Oh, yes, I was forgetting that headache!

EVE: See you later, Pearl.

Door opens and closes.

A pause.

Telephone rings.

PEARL: (*Lifting receiver*) La Boutique … Oh, good morning, Mrs Lacey … No, Mrs Bristol isn't here … Can I take a message … Four o'clock instead of two? … Yes, that'll be perfectly all right … No, no, that's quite convenient … Yes, I'll tell her …

149

Yes, we did – we managed to get the material after all. Thank you … Goodbye … (*Replaces receiver*)

Door opens.

ROBERT: Good morning …

PEARL: Oh, hello! I'm afraid you've missed Eve, she's gone out to lunch.

ROBERT: Oh – well, it doesn't matter, it's not important.

PEARL: I'm surprised you didn't see her. She only went out a moment ago.

ROBERT: (*Hesitant*) As a matter of fact, it's really you I wanted to see, Pearl.

PEARL: Well – be warned! I'm not in a very good temper this morning, so tread carefully.

ROBERT: I always tread carefully with you, Pearl. I wouldn't dare do otherwise.

PEARL: (*Amused*) You didn't tread carefully the other night, you were bloody rude!

ROBERT: So were you!

PEARL: Yes. (*Suddenly; laughing*) Yes, so I was – come to think of it. Now what can I do for you?

ROBERT: I'd like to ask you one or two questions.

PEARL: Surprise – surprise! Don't you ever get tired of asking questions?

ROBERT: I get very tired of some of the answers.

PEARL: Yes, I'll bet. Well – what is it you want to know?

ROBERT: I want to talk to you about Eve – and I want you to be very frank with me.

PEARL: I'm always frank; it's a speciality of mine. In fact, one of my dearest friends once said I wasn't a woman at all, I was just a blunt instrument. (*Robert laughs*) What about Eve? What can I tell you about her that you don't already know?

ROBERT: Did she ever talk to you about Lewis?

150

PEARL: When we first met she never talked about anything else.

ROBERT: When you first met?

PEARL: Yes – she hadn't got over the divorce and she was still intensely bitter about the whole business.

ROBERT: You mean – she felt angry with Lewis because …

PEARL: (*Irritated*) Look, you know how she felt, Robert! You and Katherine were both very friendly with her when the divorce went through.

ROBERT: Pearl … Lewis was my brother and in spite of all his faults – and God knows he had plenty – I was still very fond of him. Eve knew that at the time of the divorce, she still knows it …

PEARL: In other words, you don't think she's ever really told you the truth about her feelings towards him?

ROBERT: (*Thoughtfully*) I don't know whether she's told me the truth or not. Perhaps she has, perhaps I'm just … What I want is your impression, Pearl. <u>Your</u> feelings, based quite simply on what she's told <u>you</u> – nothing else.

PEARL: (*After a pause*) Well – I've never really believed in this so-called love-hate relationship. I've read books about it, I've seen movies about it, but – until I met Eve I always thought it was just a load of nonsense. I'm one of those people who – if I hate anybody, I hate 'em, that's it, to hell with 'em, they can take a running jump … But Eve – I must admit she's different. She used to talk about Lewis as if she were still absolutely crazy about him, and then … at other times … it was pretty obvious that she just hated his guts.

ROBERT: I see. Thank you, Pearl. That's what I wanted to know.

151

PEARL: Now may I ask you the sixty-four-thousand-dollar question?

ROBERT: I'm not sure what the sixty-four-thousand-dollar question is, but go ahead.

PEARL: Could Lewis have been killed – murdered – by a woman?

ROBERT: (*After a moment*) Yes. Yes, I think so. And so does Inspector Daly. A strong, determined sort of woman could easily have taken Lewis by surprise …

PEARL: A strong, determined sort of woman? That doesn't sound like Eve! It sounds more like me!

ROBERT: (*Laughing*) Well – you said it, Pearl!

Fade in Music.

Fade Music.

Fade in: sound of electric razor.

Telephone bell ringing.

Electric razor stops: telephone receiver lifted.

ROBERT: (*On phone*) Hello? …

EVE: (*On the other end*) Is that you, Robert?

ROBERT: Oh, hello Eve!

EVE: It's been ringing for ages, I thought you were all out.

ROBERT: No; Mrs Webb's in her room and I was shaving.

EVE: I'm sorry I missed you this morning. Was it important?

ROBERT: No – I was just passing and I thought I'd drop in on you, that's all.

EVE: You should have joined me for lunch. I was just round the corner – where we had coffee that morning. You remember …

ROBERT: Yes, I remember. I never thought of it.

A pause.

152

EVE:	Are you doing anything this evening?
ROBERT:	(*Hesitant*) No – nothing special.
EVE:	Well, why not come round for a drink?
ROBERT:	Thank you, Eve.
EVE:	Or, better still – let me take you out to dinner for a change. You're always taking me out.
ROBERT:	Well –
EVE:	Let's meet at Waldo's, in Greek Street?
ROBERT:	Yes, all right.
EVE:	Half past seven?
ROBERT:	I'll be there.
EVE:	(*Surprised*) You don't sound very enthusiastic!
ROBERT:	I'm sorry, Eve – I was just thinking, that's all. Yes, that's all right. That's fine. Half past seven. See you then … (*Replaces receiver*)

Robert continues using electric razor.

A pause.

Door opens.

MRS WEBB:	Inspector Daly's here, sir. He'd like to have a word with you.
ROBERT:	(*Stopping razor*) Yes, of course. Tell him to come in! (*Calling*) Come along in, Eric!
MRS WEBB:	I take it you're going to be in for a meal this evening, sir?
ROBERT:	Oh, Lord! No, I'm sorry, Mrs Webb. I'm going out.
MRS WEBB:	Oh dear! I wish you'd told me before, sir!
ROBERT:	I didn't know myself until a minute ago. Mrs Bristol's just invited me out to dinner.
MRS WEBB:	(*Peeved*) I wish she'd phone earlier, sir – that's all I can say!
ROBERT:	Hello, Eric! Come along in! I'm sorry, Mrs Webb.

153

Door closes.

DALY: What's eating her?

ROBERT: She thought I was going to be in for a meal and I'm not. I'm going out with Mrs Bristol.

DALY: Where?

ROBERT: (*Surprised by the question*) Where? To a little restaurant in Greek Street; it's called Waldo's. Why do you ask?

DALY: We might want to get in touch with you, Robert.

ROBERT: Why should you want to get in touch with me?

DALY: Something's happened since I saw you last.

ROBERT: (*Suddenly*) Owen! He's talked!

DALY: That's right.

ROBERT: (*Delighted*) Good for you, Eric! What happened? What made him change his mind?

DALY: Well – I know I shouldn't have done it, but – I told Dave Reece to have a chat with him.

ROBERT: Oh. My God, now you're in trouble!

DALY: No, no, it's all right. Dave was very gentlemanly, very friendly, he just quietly reasoned with Owen and …

ROBERT: Eric, for God's sake, you're not talking to the A.C. – not yet!

DALY: (*Laughing*) Don't worry, Robert – it'll be all right. Anyway, officially you're still on leave, so you won't carry the can.

ROBERT: What did Owen tell you?

DALY: Apparently May found out that Mrs Nelson was going to see you and he told Owen and Newton to stop her.

ROBERT: But how did Winter fit into the picture?

DALY: Owen's not sure, but he thinks May had a row with him and finally decided …

ROBERT: To kill two birds with one stone?

DALY: Yes; May told Winter that Mrs Nelson was a blackmailer and she'd suddenly become very curious about La Boutique. He advised Winter to talk to her, personally, and try to find out what she was up to. Winter fell for it, not realising, of course …

ROBERT: That the whole thing was a set-up, to get rid of him as well as Elka Nelson?

DALY: Yes.

ROBERT: Tell me: will Owen stick by his statement?

DALY: In my opinion, yes.

ROBERT: You're sure?

DALY: Yes, I'm sure.

ROBERT: Then there's only one thing to do, Eric. Get a warrant out for Carl May.

Fade in Music.

Fade Music.

Fade in: background noises of Savaranda Club;
People dancing; small orchestra playing.

PETERS: So this is the Savaranda Club … I've always wanted to see the inside of this place, sir. Pal of mine once won a hundred and fifty quid in a joint like this.

DALY: He was lucky. That chap over there, Peters … Isn't it Brian Wade?

PETERS: Yes.

DALY: He used to work at the Paradiso?

PETERS: That's right.

DALY: How long's he been working for May?

PETERS: About six months, I think. He's the Front of House man. Terrible gambler, but not a bad chap really.

DALY: Let's have a word with him.

155

A pause.

DALY: Excuse me, sir – we're looking for Mr May.

WADE: Have you an appointment with him?

DALY: Yes – but he doesn't know about it.

WADE: What do you mean he ... I've seen you before somewhere, haven't I?

DALY: I'm Chief-Inspector Daly ...

WADE: Of course! I thought I recognised you. What can I do for you, Inspector?

DALY: I've told you – I'm looking for Mr May.

WADE: Carl's busy right now, he always is this time of night. If there's anything I can do ...

DALY: Wade, I'm here on business, now take me up to May's office, there's a good chap.

WADE: (*Hesitating; then:*) Yes, okay, Inspector. Come this way! He's on the first floor ...

Fade music and club noises to background.

Fade in: knock on a door. Door opens.

CARL: What is it, Brian? I thought I told you ... Why, hello, Inspector! Come along in ...

DALY: Thank you, Wade – you can leave us.

Door closes.

CARL: To what do I owe this unexpected visit, Inspector?

DALY: To this piece of paper, sir.

CARL: (*Puzzled*) What do you mean?

DALY: I don't have to tell you who I am, sir – and this is a colleague of mine, Detective-Sergeant Peters. We have a warrant for your arrest, sir.

CARL: My arrest?

DALY: Yes, sir. We have good reason to believe that you're concerned with the illegal distribution of narcotics, and in this connection ...

CARL: (*Angry*) Look – cut the stage directions! What the hell is this? What's the charge?

DALY: The charge is that – together with Terence James Newton and William Henry Owen – you were responsible for the murder of an American citizen by the name of Rolf Winter. And I must warn you that anything you say …

CARL: There's only one thing I'm going to say, Inspector – this idiotic joke's gone far enough!

DALY: This isn't a joke, sir – and you know it isn't. Now if you'll be good enough to accompany me to the station.

CARL: Wait a minute! (*Picks up telephone*) I'm not accompanying you anywhere, not until I've spoken to my solicitor. (*Starts to dial*)

DALY: (*To Peters; with authority*) Tell Burton and Steele to come into the club and wait for us downstairs.

PETERS: Yes, sir.

CARL: Where do you propose taking me?

DALY: To Savile Row, sir.

CARL: (*On phone*) Who is that? … Mrs Hudson? … This is Carl May … Is your husband in? … Well please get in touch with him at once and tell him to get down to Savile Row Police Station straight away! … Yes, it would appear to be urgent, Mrs Hudson – I've been arrested!

Fade in Music.
Fade Music.

WAITER: (*Fade in*) Mrs Bristol's in the alcove, sir.

ROBERT: Oh, thank you.

A slight pause.

EVE: Hello, Robert!

ROBERT: Hello, Eve! Am I late?

EVE:	No, I was early for a change! I've ordered you a gin and tonic, is that all right?
ROBERT:	Yes, that's fine. (*Sitting down*) But look, this is on me because …
EVE:	Now don't you start that nonsense! I invited you and you accepted!
ROBERT:	(*Laughing*) Yes, all right. This is all very nice and cosy, Eve. Did you ask for the alcove?
EVE:	Yes, I did. But don't let it give you ideas. I'm sorry I missed you this morning. Why didn't you come to the café?
ROBERT:	I was hoping Pearl would be at lunch and we could have a quiet little chat. When I discovered she wasn't I pretended she was the person I wanted to see, not you.
EVE:	(*Puzzled*) But why did you do that?
ROBERT:	(*After a moment*) Eve, I'm going to tell you something and I'm afraid you're in for quite a shock.
EVE:	(*Puzzled*) Something about … Pearl?
ROBERT:	Yes – about Pearl … and Lewis … and the man who was shot, Rolf Winter.
EVE:	Go on, Robert.
ROBERT:	After the Chelsea incident – after Rolf Winter was shot – I went to Claridge's to break the news to his wife. (*Start Fade*) I had a feeling – call it a hunch if you like – that once she got over the shock Virginia Winter would tell me the truth about her husband and what happened in San Francisco. I was right.

Complete Fade.

VIRGINIA:	(*Fade in*) … What – what is it you want to know?

ROBERT:	Did you deliberately get friendly with my brother that night, at the party? Was it all prearranged – part of a plan?
VIRGINIA:	Yes.

A pause.

ROBERT:	Well – when are you going to tell me about it, Mrs Winter?
VIRGINIA:	(*Tensely*) Oh, please, please don't call me Mrs Winter. Yes, I'll tell you about it. I'll tell you all about Lewis and … what happened in San Francisco. (*A pause*) Rolf Winter wasn't a businessman, not in the strict sense of the word. And, incidentally, he wasn't my husband. His money came from the sale of narcotics. About a year or so ago he decided to extend his activities to London, and with this in mind he got in touch with a man called Carl May. To cut a long story short: May and Rolf failed to reach an agreement, and finally out of desperation, Rolf made a deal with someone else instead – someone you know, Pearl Mortimer.
ROBERT:	What do you mean – made a deal?
VIRGINIA:	I mean, she's been working for Rolf and using La Boutique as her headquarters.
ROBERT:	And Eve – Mrs Bristol?
VIRGINIA:	She knows nothing about this; she hasn't a clue as to what's been going on. In fact, when Carl May heard about La Boutique he told Rolf that unless he was cut in on the deal he'd tell Eve the whole story.
ROBERT:	Go on …
VIRGINIA:	Finally, although they never trusted each other, Rolf and Carl May came to an

	agreement. Part of this agreement was that Eve should be murdered and Lewis arrested for murder.
ROBERT:	Lewis? That was May's idea …
VIRGINIA:	Yes. To start the ball rolling a man called John C. Reynolds spun your brother a story about Rolf and a possible film proposition. You know what happened.
ROBERT:	When Lewis arrived in San Francisco you were told to get friendly with him and talk him into coming to London?
VIRGINIA:	Yes; but at the last moment I got cold feet, told Rolf I wasn't having anything to do with it, and … disappeared.
ROBERT:	(*Quietly; reproachful*) But not for long, Virginia.
VIRGINIA:	What do you mean?
ROBERT:	You didn't disappear for long.
VIRGINIA:	(*Tensely*) How could I? Don't you understand – don't you realise … Rolf had something I wanted. Something I needed, desperately. Besides I was frightened of him. One of my best friends – a girl called Suki Talmadge – had already been murdered, just because she'd been helping me.

A pause.

| ROBERT: | Go on, Virginia. |
| VIRGINIA: | After we'd been in London a few days I suddenly saw an article about Lewis is one of the newspapers. I was surprised; I didn't even realise he was in Europe. I telephoned his hotel and we … met in a coffee bar near Fleet Street. I told him everything, Robert. About |

	Rolf, about Carl May, about the photographs, about La Boutique … everything.
ROBERT:	And did you also, by any chance, give him a belt – off a dress?
VIRGINIA:	Yes, I did. I gave him the belt and the photograph.
ROBERT:	Why?
VIRGINIA:	I felt that they would prove to him that I was telling the truth. You see … Look, let me tell you how Pearl Mortimer operates. If you're a "pusher", a "courier" – a person who makes a living out of peddling drugs – then you get hold of a photograph of La Boutique and send a girl friend along to see Pearl Mortimer. The girl identifies herself with the photograph and Pearl sells her a dress with a belt on it. A few days later, after Rolf's people have vetted the "peddler", the girl takes the belt back to the shop and complains about the buckle. When the buckle's returned to her …
ROBERT:	There's a supply of heroin in it.
VIRGINIA:	Yes.
ROBERT:	It's as simple as that?
VIRGINIA:	Yes, as simple as that.
ROBERT:	But wasn't there some confusion on one occasion – didn't Winter telephone from San Francisco?
VIRGINIA:	Yes, he did, and he thought he was talking to Pearl. When he realised he wasn't – and that luckily it wasn't Eve on the phone either – the last thing he wanted to do was to arouse anyone else's suspicions. So he just let the matter drop and rang off.

ROBERT: Oh, I see … Now, tell me, and this is important: did Lewis believe your story? Did he believe what you told him?

VIRGINIA: I don't know. I think perhaps he believed part of it, but … I don't think he really understood what Rolf was like. I had the feeling all the time that he thought it would be dead easy to out-smart him.

ROBERT: (*Thoughtfully*) Knowing Lewis, I can believe that. Virginia, was it you who warned Mrs Bristol – who telephoned her flat that morning?

VIRGINIA: Yes, it was. I'd overheard a conversation between Winter and Carl May and knew what had happened. Thank God someone was there when I phoned.

ROBERT: But why didn't you get in touch with me earlier? You knew that Lewis had a brother at Scotland Yard, so surely …

VIRGINIA: I tried to. I rang the Yard the moment we arrived, before I knew Lewis was in London in fact. They told me you were in Venice, staying with your sister. In the end I decided the only thing to do was to write to you about Pearl Mortimer and La Boutique. I put one of the photographs in an envelope and was actually writing the letter when Rolf came into the lounge. He stood by the desk saying goodbye to a friend of his. I was terrified in case he realised what I was doing. Finally, I stuck the envelope down just as it was, and handed it to the hall porter.

ROBERT: I see.

VIRGINIA: Later, when I heard you were back in London, I called round to see you, but you were out.

ROBERT: Yes, I know. You saw Katherine. You told her that, in your opinion, it was Carl May who killed Lewis.

VIRGINIA: No, that's not strictly true. I simply told her what happened in San Francisco.

ROBERT: But you think May did kill him?

VIRGINIA: (*Thoughtfully*) I think he must have done.

ROBERT: (*Suddenly; putting his glass down*) Well – thank you for the drink.

VIRGINIA: If there's anything you'd like me to do before I return to the States ...

ROBERT: My colleague, Inspector Daly, will want you to make a statement, of course, but ... Yes, quite apart from that, there is something I want you to do. A friend of mine, a Dr Stuart Haimes, has opened a clinic just outside Scarborough. I'd like to think you were prepared to go up there and stay with him for a couple of months.

VIRGINIA: (*After a moment*) I'm sorry, Robert.

ROBERT: You mean – you refuse? You don't want to?

VIRGINIA: (*Almost irritated*) It isn't that I refuse, it isn't that I don't want to, it's ... Well, I hate to disillusion you, but – I've tried that sort of thing before. Twice. Once in Chicago and once in New Orleans.

ROBERT: I want you to try it again. Here – now – in England.

VIRGINIA: (*Start Fade*) I'll think about it.

ROBERT: (*With authority; almost rude*) I don't want you to think about it, Virginia! I want you to do it!

Complete Fade.

163

EVE: (*Fade in*) …Robert, I didn't know about Pearl … I swear to you I didn't! Why even now … I can hardly believe it. You mean she's been using me – using the shop – all this time?

ROBERT: Yes, and not only that, but when I became curious she even started to throw suspicion on to you.

EVE: But when did you first suspect her?

ROBERT: She made one or two mistakes. There was the belt, for instance, and her reference to the girl on the phone. You didn't tell her it was a girl who tipped me off that morning, you couldn't have done because you didn't know. I simply told you that "someone" had telephoned.

EVE: And the belt?

ROBERT: You remember the belt you gave me for Katherine? Pearl thought you'd made a mistake and got hold of one of hers – one with heroin in it. When we went out to have a coffee that morning I left my suitcase behind in the shop and …

EVE: Pearl took the belt.

ROBERT: Yes.

EVE: Robert, tell me: why did May want the letter that Lewis had written?

ROBERT: I think Lewis must have known something about May, something that had happened in the past, and May was frightened that Lewis was going to pass this information on to Winter. In actual fact, after his talk with Virginia, Lewis was only interested in one thing.

EVE: Which was to get Virginia away from Winter?

ROBERT: Yes – hence the note to Winter with my name on it.

EVE: (*Suddenly*) Robert, isn't that the Inspector?

ROBERT: Yes, it is. (*Raising his voice*) Eric, we're over here! In the alcove!

DALY: (*Approaching*) I'm sorry, I didn't see you. Good evening, Mrs Bristol.

EVE: Good evening.

ROBERT: What's happened, Eric?

DALY: We picked up May and we've charged him. He's at the station at the moment waiting for his solicitor to show up. Mrs Bristol, I've applied for a warrant to search La Boutique. I haven't been able to pick it up yet, but if we have your permission we could go straight ahead.

EVE: Yes, of course, Inspector. In fact we can go there now if you like.

DALY: I ... think perhaps it might be a good idea if you left this to us, Mrs Bristol.

ROBERT: Yes, I agree. We'll meet later at your place, Eve.

EVE: Yes, all right, Robert. (*Start Fade*) Here we are, Inspector – here's the keys to the shop. There's two; one's for the mortise lock.

DALY: Thank you, Mrs Bristol.

Complete Fade.

Fade in: sound of police car.
Background of traffic.

DALY: I should pull up on the corner, Colman.

COLMAN: Yes sir.

Car draws in to kerb.
Car doors open; passengers get out.

DALY: Is there another entrance to the shop?

ROBERT: Yes, there's a tradesmen's entrance at the side.

DALY: Right. Lever, I want you and Beckett to watch both entrances. If anyone comes out – stop them.

LEVER: Yes, sir.

DALY: The Superintendent and I will …

ROBERT: (*Stopping him*) Wait a minute!

DALY: What is it?

A pause.

LEVER: There's someone coming out of the shop now, sir.

BECKETT: Yes, there is, sir …

Another pause.

ROBERT: It's Miss Mortimer …

DALY: (*Quietly*) She's seen you, Robert.

LEVER: (*A moment*) Yes, I think she has, sir.

DALY: What the devil is she doing at the shop at this time of night?

ROBERT: Someone must have tipped her off. Did Carl May make a phone call by any chance?

DALY: Only to his solicitor and he wasn't at home … Oh, my God! It was a woman May spoke to on the phone! I'll bet he pulled a fast one on me!

LEVER: She's going back into the shop, sir!

ROBERT: Come along, Eric!

DALY: (*Quickly; Start Fade*) Lever … Beckett … cover the shop … Quickly, Robert …

Complete Fade.

Fade in: key being inserted in lock.

Shop door refuses to open.

DALY: She's jammed the lock!

ROBERT: No, I don't think so …

DALY: Yes, she has … I can tell by … No, you're right – the lock's all right – there's just something against the door …

ROBERT: Push, Eric … that's it … Push …

Door partly opens.

DALY: It's only a chair …

Chair tumbles over as the door is pushed open and Robert and Daly quickly enter the shop.

ROBERT: She's not here – she must be down … (*Suddenly*) Pearl!

PEARL: (*Tensely*) Stand back! Get away from that door!

ROBERT: Pearl, don't be a fool – put that gun down …

PEARL: You heard what I said! …

DALY: Now, Miss Mortimer, please don't be stupid.

PEARL: I warn you – if you come a step nearer I shall fire!

ROBERT: Stay where you are, Eric! I have a feeling Miss Mortimer means business – and not for the first time either, unless I'm mistaken.

PEARL: Go down the stairs to the basement!

ROBERT: You killed Lewis – didn't you, Pearl?

PEARL: You heard what I said – both of you, go down the stairs … to the basement …

ROBERT: (*Moving towards her*) Supposing we don't, Pearl? Supposing we …

PEARL: (*Desperate*) I'll give you five seconds – just five seconds – and if you don't do as I tell you by then …

ROBERT: Look out, Eric!

As Robert speaks he dives at Pearl shouting
"Get the gun! Get the gun, Eric!"
There is a short, tense struggle, then the gun fires;
The bullet smashing into the shop window.

ROBERT: (*Alarmed*) Are you all right?

DALY: Yes, the bullet hit the window and … Stop her! Stop her, Robert!

The shop door slams.

ROBERT: Come on, Eric!

Fade in: street noises.

Lever's voice shouting: "Stop her, Beckett! Look out! … Watch that car!"

As Lever shouts we hear the sound of an approaching car, quickly followed by the sudden screeching of brakes.

ROBERT: (*Softly*) Oh … my God …

Fade.

Fade in: excited voices, quickly gathering crowd to scene of street accident.

DALY: What happened, Beckett?

BECKETT: She ran right across the road … I don't think she even saw the car …

LEVER: She couldn't have done, she ran straight into it …

DALY: Here's the Superintendent.

BECKETT: How is she, sir?

ROBERT: I don't think you'll have to worry about a warrant, Eric. Beckett, go and have a word with the driver of the car – he's in a hell of a state, poor devil. Tell him not to worry, we've half a dozen witnesses to prove it wasn't his fault.

BECKETT: Yes, sir.

Sound of approaching ambulance.

DALY: Here's the ambulance.

Fade in ambulance.

Fade in Music

Fade Music.

ROBERT: (*Fade in*) … She died just as the ambulance reached the hospital.

EVE: (*Softly*) Oh, Robert …

ROBERT: She had a large supply of heroin in her handbag, she'd obviously been warned to get it out of the shop.

168

EVE: I knew nothing about this drug business ... I swear to you, Robert; I hadn't the slightest idea that Pearl was mixed up in it.

ROBERT: (*Stopping her*) I know, Eve. There's no need for you to worry, my dear ... Pearl made a statement to Eric just before she died ...

EVE: Did she mention Lewis at all? Did she say what happened that night?

ROBERT: Yes. Winter was angry because Virginia had contacted Lewis and he told Pearl to get rid of him. She sent Lewis a message asking him to call at La Boutique – a message which he thought came from you, Eve.

EVE: Oh ... (*Softly*) Oh, I see.

A pause.

ROBERT: You look tired, my dear. If I were you, I'd go to bed.

EVE: No ... No, I'm all right. Shall I make some coffee?

ROBERT: Yes, yes, that's a good idea.

EVE: What are you going to do now, Robert – return to Venice and finish your holiday?

ROBERT: No, I don't think so, there's still an awful lot to do here.

EVE: But not for you, surely – you're still on leave.

ROBERT: Technically, yes.

EVE: Well, if I were you, I'd go straight back to Katherine's.

ROBERT: If you ask me, you're the one that needs a holiday, Eve – not me.

EVE: No ...

ROBERT: (*A sudden thought*) Look – you think I need a holiday and I think you need one, so why don't we both go to Venice? I'm sure Katherine and Freddie would love to have us.

EVE: It wouldn't be any use, Robert.

ROBERT: Why not?

EVE: We'd just sit and talk … about Pearl … and Lewis … and what happened at La Boutique.

ROBERT: Yes – we might. On the other hand, we might not. Venice is an unusual place, Eve. It certainly has a very unusual effect on me. I can be very persuasive in Venice.

EVE: (*After a pause; quite serious*) How persuasive, Robert?

ROBERT: Well – I might persuade you to forget La Boutique, for instance. And if I'm lucky – dead lucky – and the sun's shining … who knows … I might even persuade you to forget Lewis.

Fade in Music.
Fade Music.

THE END

The Press Pack

… press cuttings about *La Boutique*

Did you ever hear how Francis Durbridge nearly put the cinemas out of business in Germany? Well, it is true. It happened when one of his serials – it might have been "*Tim Frazer*" or "*Melissa*" or "*Bat Out of Hell*" – was running on television. Everyone stayed at home to watch. "I've been quite embarrassed myself," says Durbridge: "all the taxis were off the street." And that not only in Germany, but in France, Italy, Scandinavia – all over Europe. In this country, of course, we have known what it is to be hooked on a Durbridge serial ever since the first Paul Temple serial on radio in 1938.

And so when the European Broadcasting Union for the first time came to choose someone to write a radio play for the networks of the associated countries, Francis Durbridge picked himself. The outcome is "*La Boutique*." Incidentally it is one of the last productions before he retires of Martyn C. Webster, who has produced all of the Paul Temple serials since 1938.

"*La Boutique*" is a word which – like "Durbridge" – means the same all over the Continent. It is the name of the dress shop kept by Eve, the divorced wife of Lewis Bristol, who is a songwriter with an international reputation. Lewis is at the moment in Los Angeles, but after an extremely frustrating and mysterious experience with an extremely fascinating girl (Lewis is like that) at a millionaire's party, he comes to England to have a word with his brother, Superintendent Robert Bristol of Scotland Yard. Robert, however, is not interested; he is on leave, and he is going to stay with their sister in Venice. But no sooner has he got there than Durbridge-type things begin to happen in London …

You can't really call a Durbridge serial a Whodunnit – it's more of a "What's-going-on-here?" Every episode ends with a new mystery – except the last; and every episode seems to tidy up the previous mystery but in time to face you with another. Try the first episode, and you have to make a date with the second; listen to two and you are as hooked as those Hamburg taxi-drivers.

But do not be deterred. "*La Boutique*" will not keep you from your Christmas shopping. The story is told in five episodes at the rate of two a week, on Monday and Thursday evenings. In fifteen days' time you will know just what La Boutique had to do with Los Angeles and Venice.

Radio Times

Francis Durbridge, author of many BBC radio and television serials will write the first radio play to be commissioned by the European Broadcasting Union. It will be called "*La Boutique.*"

The play is a thriller serialised in five, 30-minute episodes. It will be broadcast exclusively by the participating countries during a two-year period starting in May, 1987.

The BBC Light Programme will broadcast it for British listeners. It is an adventure story with an international background, designed to appeal to radio audiences in many different countries among them, Britain, Austria, Italy, Germany, Belgium, Norway, Sweden, Switzerland, Turkey, Greece, Finland, Canada, South Africa and Australia.

Francis Durbridge is the creator of "*Paul Temple,*" central character in the long running radio series, whose adventures are still being followed by listeners in many countries overseas.

Durbridge's radio and TV serials have been broadcast in BBC and locally produced versions by very many stations all over the world with success. On TV the BBC has presented thirteen adventure serials by Durbridge including "*The World of Tim Frazer*" and "*Melissa*".

Southern Evening Echo

The European Broadcasting Union has commissioned Francis Durbridge, author of many BBC serials, to write the first radio play to be broadcast in a two-year period in countries which are members of the union.

The play, "*La Boutique*" an adventure story with an international background, will be serialised in five half-hour episodes by the broadcasting organisations throughout Europe from next May. The BBC Light Programme will transmit it for British listeners.

Mr Durbridge is the creator of "*Paul Temple*," central character in the long-running radio series. Many of his radio and TV serials have been broadcast by stations all over the world. His TV serials have included "*The World of Tim Frazer*" and "*Melissa*."

The Daily Telegraph

Thirty years ago – in 1938 – an elegant and ingenious character called Paul Temple was introduced to listeners and he immediately became a public hero. His creator was a young Yorkshire author, Francis Durbridge, and his first serial was given to Martyn C. Webster to produce. That partnership has persisted and has become one of the greatest success stories on radio. Paul Temple is not only the favourite detective of generations of listeners here, but his fame has spread all over the world and his adventures have been translated into many languages. On the eve of his retirement from BBC staff, Mr Webster received an appropriate surprise. "We'd been trying to get Durbridge to write another Paul Temple story for ages," Mr Webster says (the last was in 1965) "and just before I was due to leave, he handed me the new manuscript with a grin. I was delighted, and I think it's one of the best he's done." It begins on February 28th. Durbridge is adept at creating situations which finish excitingly. He creates characters you can believe in – not cardboard people – and he goes to great trouble to verify every single detail. Durbridge's success goes on: "*La*

Boutique" which started a new pattern of twice-weekly serials at the opening of BBC's Radio 1 and 2 will be repeated shortly, and his stories have been equally successful on television – the latest being "*Bat Out of Hell*."

The Cork Examiner

In that uneasy peace between the wars a Yorkshire-born student sat down and wrote a sketch for a university revue. He took part in the show when it was broadcast, but is the first to agree that he was a better author than actor.

Today Francis Durbridge is an international figure in the world of television – possibly a unique one. His immaculately written thrillers are created with such skill that viewers in a score of countries wait on tenterhooks for the answer to the key question: "Who killed –?"

He is par excellence, a weaver of mystery, holding together a dozen tangled threads which he alone can unravel with devasting effect – and his stories, ingenious and inventive, have overcome the language barrier.

What is more, he still sees a future for this type of entertainment. "If your scripts are up to date, if the stories move along at a good pace, and you have interesting characters there is always a market for this kind of thing," he told me.

Thirty years have passed since Durbridge brought to life his famous detective, Paul Temple, the elegant, debonair man who, behind that suave exterior, moves implacably towards the eleventh-hour triumph of justice over villainy. Now, a new twice-weekly serial is on the air on BBC Radio 2's "*Paul Temple and the Alex Affair*."

Thus Durbridge has returned to his first love, radio, while recently on television "*Bat Out of Hell*" showed a different audience that the old magic had not lost its power.

His serial "*La Boutique*" will shortly be given an encore and it is a measure of the author's standing in Europe that when the European Broadcasting Commission decided for the

174

first time to buy a play for its network of associated countries, Durbridge was the man who got the job.

It has already been said that Durbridge was the writer who put the cinemas out of business in West Germany with his "*Melissa*" and now "*La Boutique*" was to be produced not only in Britain, but in Austria, Italy, Germany, Belgium, Norway, Sweden, Turkey, Switzerland, Greece and Finland, and in the Commonwealth countries as well.

Now in his mid-fifties, Francis Durbridge lives and writes with professional application for a regular period each day – his unshakable target to keep an audience of many millions guessing.

His manner is mild, and, though he enjoys a happy family life, and the prosperity success has brought him, he avoids with genuine modesty that double-edged weapon of the ambitious, publicity. To talk to Durbridge about his career and beliefs is in itself a major achievement.

He was born in Hull, and, though he claims to have forgotten what it was about, his first mystery play was written and produced while he was still at school. The true turning point came when he was studying, with modified enthusiasm, at Birmingham University. A novice revue sketch caught the ear of Martyn C. Webster, a BBC producer.

"Martyn, who liked the sketch, asked me to write something else for radio. I fancy he rather expected more revue material, but instead I sent him a full-length play called "*Promotion*", which was about life in a department store."

Webster was impressed by the play and put it on the air. So began a producer-author partnership which has lasted more than thirty years.

By one of life's remarkable coincidences, one actress who was in "*Promotion*" was Marjorie Westbury, who has been Paul Temple's wife, the unflappable Steve, in almost all the Temple serials. She has out-stayed quite a number of Temples.

Durbridge wrote many more plays for radio drama. Then he came to the conclusion that it was all very well for broadcasting to adapt tales of the classic detectives in fiction, radio should have its own counterpart.

Before long the first serial "*Send For Paul Temple*" was heard throughout the land. When it ended there were more than 7,000 letters from listeners asking for more. Since then Temple has been the hero of books, films, short stories and strip-cartoons.

"No, he has never been on television," his creator told me. He prefers as a matter of policy to portray other detective characters for the screen.

I left Francis Durbridge working on yet another television show.

Scarborough Evening News